"Do you have a spare pillow and blanket?"
Spence asked.

"I knew it!" Tricia said, leaning against the dresser. "I just knew it. This is where you tell me you're spending the night on my sofa."

"Bingo," he said, a teasing look in his eyes.

"Why?"

"Why?" He shook his head. "Your favorite question. Because you've had a tough day with all that's happened, and you might have nightmares or something. I want to be here if you need me, Tricia. Pretend you won me in a raffle, honey, because I'm staying."

"That's ridiculous," she said, her voice trembling at the man's closeness. "You can't sleep here. I won't be able to sleep if you're sleeping here. I've never had a man sleep here, so you can't, you just can't sleep here!"

"Want to try that a little slower?"

"Go home, Lieutenant! That's an order."

"Sorry, ma'am," he said, grinning. "I'm in one of my 'above and beyond the call of duty' modes. I'm here to protect you from all and everything."

"Ah, but, Lieutenant," Tricia said softly, "who is going to protect you from *me*?"

Bantam Books by Joan Elliott Pickart
Ask your bookseller for the titles you have missed.

WHAT ARE *LOVESWEPT* ROMANCES?

They are stories of true romance and touching emotion. We believe those two very important ingredients are constants in our highly sensual and very believable stories in the *LOVESWEPT* line. Our goal is to give you, the reader, stories of consistently high quality that may sometimes make you laugh, sometimes make you cry, but are always fresh and creative and contain many delightful surprises within their pages.

Most romance fans read an enormous number of books. Those they truly love, they keep. Others may be traded with friends and soon forgotten. We hope that each *LOVESWEPT* romance will be a treasure—a "keeper." We will always try to publish

*LOVE STORIES YOU'LL NEVER FORGET
BY AUTHORS YOU'LL ALWAYS REMEMBER*

The Editors

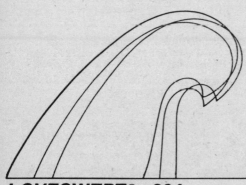

LOVESWEPT® • 204

Joan Elliott Pickart
Reforming Freddy

BANTAM BOOKS
TORONTO • NEW YORK • LONDON • SYDNEY • AUCKLAND

REFORMING FREDDY

A Bantam Book / August 1987

*If you would be interested in receiving protective vinyl
covers for your Loveswept books, please write to this address
for information:*

> *Loveswept*
> *Bantam Books*
> *P.O. Box 985*
> *Hicksville, NY 11802*

ISBN 0-553-21827-1

Published simultaneously in the United States and Canada

PRINTED IN THE UNITED STATES OF AMERICA

O   0 9 8 7 6 5 4 3 2 1

For my daughters,
who have given me so many lovely
memories to keep

One

It had seemed like a good idea at the time.

When Tricia Todd had entered the lobby of the high-rise building that housed her office, she immediately saw the throng of people waiting for the elevators. It was the early morning crush, and Tricia wrinkled her nose in distaste at the prospect of the usual jostling and jockeying for position.

She would, she decided, walk up the stairs to her fourth floor office as part of her new physical fitness program. The exercise would replace jogging, which she'd rejected flat out after one pain-ridden attempt. Jogging was definitely not her thing. She'd gotten near-crippling cramps in her calves, her heart had pounded like a jackhammer, and, oh, ugh, the sweat. Never mind that her mother had said that ladies only "glowed," as she so delicately put it. That had been sweat dripping off Tricia's body. Jogging was the pits.

And so, convinced that climbing the stairs was

a terrific idea, Tricia headed for them. She hoisted the strap of her large canvas tote bag higher on her shoulder, pushed open the fire door, and began her ascent at a brisk pace. The spike heels of her shoes clicked rhythmically on the metal steps, and the skirt of her pale sundress swirled around her knees as she made her way upward.

One flight.

So far, so good, she thought. This was a breeze. And so much more civilized than jogging. Her short dark curls were probably bouncing ridiculously on her head, but there was no one to see them. Everyone else was smushing himself into the elevators.

Two flights.

A piece of cake, Tricia told herself. This was a cinch. Well, she *was* getting a bit winded, and her throat was becoming awfully dry, and she wished she didn't have quite so much junk in her tote bag, but she was doing fine.

She stopped on the third floor landing and took a deep breath, which sounded to her like a walrus calling to its mate. She really was in rotten shape, she admitted. A physical wreck at twenty-five. But she was correcting that with her new program. There was no extra fat on her five-foot-four-inch frame, but she was mushy, had no muscle tone. She'd read about muscle tone in a magazine and had immediately decided she didn't have any. Well, she was going to tone up her muscles, by golly. Or die in the attempt.

"A butterscotch ball," she said, beginning to rummage through her bag. "That's what I need." She was very thirsty and the candy would help, and maybe the surge of sugar would propel her up the remaining flight. "I know they're in here," she muttered, digging deeper.

Her hand closed around a foreign object in the bottom of her bag, and she pulled it out. It was her nephew Tony's black plastic squirt gun. The next instant, she heard a thundering noise overhead and gasped in surprise.

With the squirt gun clutched tightly in her hand, she stared wide-eyed at the figure barreling down the stairs toward her. He was a boy of sixteen or seventeen, was wearing jeans and a T-shirt, and he was carrying a gun.

Dear heaven above, she screamed silently, he was carrying a gun!

"Damn," the youth growled when he saw her. He stopped abruptly, teetering on the stairs halfway down, and pointed the gun directly at her. "Put it down, lady," he said, his voice trembling slightly. "Drop it."

Put what down? she wondered frantically. Her tote bag? What?

"The gun, lady. Ditch it!"

Only then did Tricia realize she was pointing the squirt gun at the boy. She glanced at it, at him, then told her fingers to release their stranglehold on the plastic toy. They didn't move!

"I—" she started, only to be interrupted by another roar of noise overhead, the thudding of running feet, and the sudden appearance of a man.

He halted his descent about eight steps above the boy, and to Tricia's horror he extended his arm straight toward the teenager. Attached to the arm was a hand, and in the hand was another gun!

"I can't handle this," she mumbled, swallowing a near-hysterical giggle.

"It's over, Freddy," the man said, his voice low and menacing. "Drop it."

"No way," Freddy yelled. "You drop it, Walker, or I'll take out your sexy partner here."

Sexy partner? Tricia mused rather absently. There were more people joining this fiasco? But that kid was looking directly at her. Oh, Lord, *she* was the sexy partner. My, my, no one had ever called her sexy before.

"Give it up, Freddy," the man said in a voice so menacing and chilling that Tricia shivered.

Terrified, she swept her gaze over the tall man, taking in his light brown sun-streaked hair, the rugged, tanned features of his face, the way his black T-shirt and faded jeans molded to his tightly muscled body. Now *that*, she thought, was muscle tone. And *that* was the most masculine man she'd ever had the pleasure of feasting her eyes on.

"I'll shoot her, Walker," Freddy said.

The panic in the boy's voice snapped Tricia out of her semi-trance. Oh, for Pete's sake, she thought, this was ridiculous. Here they stood like the Three Stooges, pointing guns at one another, and hers wasn't even real. Her feet were beginning to hurt. She'd had enough of this nonsense.

"Freddy," she said, narrowing her eyes and striving for a stern tone of voice that she had a feeling was a total flop, "the jig is up, the caper is canned. Drop that gun or I'll shoot you in the . . . dingle-dangle. Go ahead. Day my make."

"Huh?" Freddy said.

"Or however that goes," she muttered.

Freddy slowly lowered his gun. "Where in the hell did you get her, Walker?" he asked, an incredulous expression on his face.

Tricia gasped as Walker moved in a smooth blur. He grabbed the gun from Freddy's hand, then hauled the boy down the stairs by the back of the T-shirt. She flattened herself against the wall, the squirt gun still tightly clutched in her hand.

"Monroe!" Walker yelled. "Jensen!"

Two uniformed police officers came running down the stairs, guns drawn.

"No more guns," Tricia said to no one. "I really would prefer it if there weren't any more guns."

"You've done it this time, Freddy," Walker said. "You've been driving us nuts with your stupid pranks, but now you've crossed over the line to where the big boys play."

"Come on, Walker," Freddy said, trying to wiggle free of the tight grasp on his shirt. "I was just messin' around, man. Check the gun, it isn't even loaded. I didn't break in here, either. I just sort of spent the night. Give me a break."

"Tell it to the judge." Walker thrust Freddy at the police officers. "Get him out of here. And take his weapon with you."

"Where are they taking me?" Freddy asked, his voice shaking.

"Juvenile Hall," Walker said.

Freddy moaned. "Oh, man, no. Walker, I swear, I'll never again—"

"Move it," Walker said.

"Okay, Lieutenant," one of the officers said. "Let's go, Freddy my boy."

" 'Bye, Freddy," Tricia said, waving her hand rather breezily.

Lieutenant Walker turned to face her. "Ma'am? Are you all right?"

"What?" she asked, looking up at him. Oh, what beautiful blue eyes, she thought dreamily. And such long eyelashes. He was so handsome, this Lieutenant Walker. If her tongue were working, she'd ask him how he'd developed such gorgeous muscle tone.

"It's a squirt gun," he said, looking down at her hand. "It's a damn toy. I can't believe this. Listen, are you okay?"

"Hmmm?"

Lieutenant Spencer Walker attempted to retrieve the squirt gun from the woman's hand, only to discover she had a viselike grip on it. He frowned as he noted her dreamy expression and crooked smile, then gently pried her fingers from around the toy.

"You don't need this anymore," he said. "Can't have you shooting anyone in the dingle-dangle."

"Hmmm?"

Damn, he thought, she was really out of it, in some kind of shock. What in hell was he going to do with her? Should he slap her to bring her back to her senses? No, he couldn't hit this delicate woman. This delicate, beautiful woman. She wasn't sophisticated-looking, but fresh, wholesome, pretty as a picture in her pink sundress. And totally spaced out at the moment. Day my make? he

thought, suddenly grinning. She was really something.

Tricia moaned silently. What a smile! Such white
teeth and . . . She really didn't feel very well. Maybe
if she had a butterscotch ball . . .

"Ma'am?" he asked, slipping his gun into the
back of his belt. "Wouldn't you like to get out of
here?" He dropped the squirt gun into her bag.
"Let's go find someplace for you to sit down. Okay,
ma'am?"

She flashed him a dazzling smile. And then
Patricia Alida Louise Todd did what any healthy,
red-blooded woman would do under the circum-
stances: She fainted.

"Oh, Lord," Spence said. His arms shot out to
catch the female bundle crumbling toward him.
He scooped her up, one arm beneath her knees,
the other around her shoulders, and held her
tightly to his chest. "Hello?" he said quietly, staring down at her.

For a long moment he didn't move, but just
gazed at the lovely woman in his arms. Her lips
were slightly parted, and he had a sudden urge to
lower his head and sample their sweetness. He
took a deep breath and his senses filled with the
aroma of soap and a delicate flowery cologne. She
was feather-light, seemed to weigh nothing at all,
and he was suddenly aware of his own size and
strength. He missed no detail of her body—the
peachy glow of her skin, her small breasts, the tiny
waist. The legs resting on his arm were slender
and shapely, and he imagined them bare. They
would be smooth as satin, and . . . A trickle of

sweat ran down his spine, and he jerked himself back to reality.

Shifting his precious cargo in his arms, he opened the door and stepped out into the carpeted corridor of the third floor, her tote bag thudding against his thighs. He entered the first office.

An elderly woman was sitting at the desk, and she gasped when she saw him.

"Police business, ma'am," he said. "Do you have a sofa where I can lay her down?"

"That dear little thing is a criminal?" the woman asked, covering her heart with her hand.

"No, she . . ." He grinned. "She's my partner. She fainted, that's all."

"Mercy," the woman said, getting to her feet. "Bring her right in here. Mr. Sivit isn't in yet."

"Appreciate it," Spence said, striding after the woman into the inner office.

He laid Tricia on a leather sofa and placed a throw pillow under her head. Sitting down next to her, he took her small hand between his two large ones. A deep frown knitted his tawny eyebrows together.

"Here's some water," the secretary said, setting a glass on the end table. "My, she's lovely. She doesn't look strong enough to be a policewoman. Oh, dear, my phone is ringing."

"You go back to whatever you were doing," Spence said. "Thanks for your help."

"Oh, you're quite welcome," she said, and hurried from the room.

"Come on, Sleeping Beauty, snap out of it,"

Spence urged. Tricia moaned. "That's it. Open those beautiful dark eyes."

Such a wonderful voice, Tricia mused. Her thoughts seemed to come from far away. It was so deep, so rich and mellow. He wanted her to open her eyes? Well, certainly. Was there anything else he wanted? She was putty in his hands, whoever he was.

She slowly lifted her lashes, blinked once, twice, then turned her head to stare into the blue, blue depths of a man's eyes. The man who was masculinity personified. The man with the marvelous muscle tone. And the gun.

"Oh!" she said, and started to sit up.

"Hey easy," the man said, gently pushing her back by the shoulders. "Let's take this nice and easy."

"Did he shoot me? Did Freddy shoot me?"

He chuckled. "No. He gave up the minute you threatened to let him have it in the dingle-dangle."

"Oh," she said, feeling a warm flush on her cheeks. "I don't usually say things like that, but I was under a bit of stress."

"Don't worry," he said, smiling. "I've heard worse. I'm Spence Walker, by the way. I'm a police officer."

"Tricia Todd. I'm a CPA."

"No kidding? You like all those numbers? My checkbook hasn't balanced in ten years. So, how are you feeling, Tricia Todd, CPA?"

"Fine."

"Good."

"I've got to get to my office."

"All right."

Neither moved, though. Their gazes held, and

Tricia became acutely aware that somehow her hand had become nestled between his. His hands were big and warm, calloused and strong, and one thumb was lightly stroking her wrist. She was also *very* aware that his muscle-toned thigh was pressed against her mushy one, creating a funny sensation in the pit of her stomach.

"You were extremely brave during that mess with Freddy," he said, his voice low.

"I was scared stiff," she said. Her own voice had a strange breathy quality.

"Would you like a drink of water?" he asked. Let go of her hand, Walker, he told himself. He would, in a minute. Damn, he wanted to kiss this woman! There was just something about her that was pulling at him like metal slivers to a magnet. What would she do if he kissed her? Hell, she'd probably haul out her squirt gun and shoot him in the dingle-dangle!

"Yes, please," she said.

"What?"

"Water."

"Oh, sure." He released her hand to reach for the glass.

Tricia pushed herself up to a sitting position and accepted the drink. The water was cool and refreshing as it slid down her parched throat. Spence Walker must have carried her in here, she realized, wherever here was. And to think she'd missed being held in those strong arms. He kept looking at her lips. Well, she'd been looking at his too. He had sensuous lips, firm and nicely shaped. What would it be like to feel them against hers? And . . .

"More?" he asked.

"Pardon me?"

"Water."

"Oh, no, that was plenty, thank you. I really must be going. I hate to sound like a cliché, but where am I?"

"Some guy's office on the second floor. Where are you supposed to be?"

"Fourth floor."

"Do you make a habit of trying to defend yourself with a squirt gun?" he asked, frowning slightly.

She laughed. "Heavens, no. I didn't even know it was in my tote bag. It belongs to my nephew, Tony. I was trying to find a butterscotch ball."

"Lieutenant," a uniformed officer said from the doorway, "I've been looking for you. Need anything else before we clear out of here?"

"No," Spence said, getting to his feet. "I'll see to Miss Todd. It is miss, isn't it?" he asked, looking back at her. Not that he was that interested, of course, he told himself.

"Yes," Tricia said. Was she imagining that he seemed very interested in her answer?

"Okay. See ya, Lieutenant," the officer said.

Tricia stood up. She glanced down at her dress to determine how wrinkled it was from her being toted around in the strong arms of Lieutenant Spence Walker.

"You look lovely," he said in a deep, rumbly voice.

She gazed up at him, and for the life of her she could not think of one thing to say. She was held immobile once again by Spence's compelling blue eyes.

A man could drown in her eyes, Spence thought. They were so big, so dark, like velvet. Lord, what a cornball thing to think. Well, what did he expect after being up half the night trying to find Freddy? He was hungry and needed some sleep. Tricia Todd wasn't all *that* terrific.

"Thank you for everything, Lieutenant," she said and smiled.

Yes, she was, Spence corrected himself. She was definitely terrific. "I didn't do anything," he said briskly. "You caught Freddy, not me. Listen, I'll have to check with the juvenile authorities to find out what kind of statement I'll need from you."

"Does Freddy really have to be locked up in Juvenile Hall?"

"They don't exactly lock them up. They just keep a very close eye on their guests. Maybe if Freddy Jackson is off the streets for a while, I can get some sleep. You said you were on the fourth floor?"

"Yes."

"I'll swing by after I do the initial paperwork on our friend Fred. Are you sure you feel steady enough to get upstairs? I'd be glad to go with you." More than glad, he added silently.

"I'm fine," she said. Why couldn't she ever lie? she wondered. Everyone she knew could lie. Darn.

Damn, he thought. "Well, okay, I'll see you later then."

"All right," she said, picking up her tote bag. "Good-bye, Lieutenant."

"It's Spence, Miss Todd."

"Please, call me Tricia. Is Spence short for Spencer?"

"Yes. Are you actually Patricia?" Good Lord, what a stupid conversation, he thought. But he didn't want her to leave!

"Yes. Patricia," she said. This was dumb. But she wanted to stay just another moment or two. Oh, for Pete's sake, enough was enough. "Well, I'm off. Thanks again." She extended her hand to him.

That was a mistake.

The whispers of heat that still lingered within Tricia from when she and Spence had been so close on the sofa burst into flame as his strong hand closed around her slender one. A trail was blazed up her arm and across her breasts, causing her nipples to grow taut and press against the lacy fabric of her bra. Then the flames spread lower, curling in her stomach and a secret place deep within her.

Spence felt as though he'd been punched in the gut as Tricia's hand melted into his. The hot, pulsing sensation beneath the zipper of his jeans told him exactly what effect Tricia was having on him. And he was only holding her hand! But before, before, he'd held her in his arms, cradled her soft, warm body close to his chest.

"This is," Tricia said, her voice barely above a whisper, "the most startling experience I've ever had."

"Freddy?" he asked, his own voice husky. He did not release her hand.

"You."

"I know. You're knocking me over here, Tricia Todd."

"So, this is lust," she said thoughtfully, slowly

pulling her hand free. "I've often wondered what it would be like."

"Lust?" he repeated, frowning.

"Fascinating. Really quite remarkable. My goodness, I've had quite a day already, and it's not even noon. Well, good-bye, Spence," she said, and started toward the door.

"Hold it just a damn minute," he said, grabbing her arm. "What's all this garbage about lust?"

"Oh, well, if you want to get ultra-polite about it, you could call it desire, I suppose. I'm sure you're used to it. You're an extremely handsome, virile man, I'd guess you do and have done unto you your fair share of lusting, or desiring, or whatever."

"That's not a very nice thing to say, Tricia," he said, narrowing his eyes.

"Oh. Well, I'm sorry. I certainly didn't mean to insult you. May I ask you a rather clinical question?"

"Why not?" he said, throwing up his hands.

"Did you just feel a funny fluttering sensation in the pit of your stomach?"

"What I felt," he said, through clenched teeth, "was located a bit lower than that. Are you for real?"

"How am I going to find out things if I don't ask? Maybe I just overreacted to you because my system is still whacky from fainting and having guns pointed at me."

"That's enough," he said, grabbing her upper arms and hauling her against him. "You reacted to *me* pure and simple. Got that? Oh, hell," he muttered, and brought his mouth down hard onto hers.

Tricia's tote bag slid to the floor with a thud and her eyes flew wide open at the shock of Spence's mouth moving roughly on hers. But in the next instant the kiss gentled, and her lashes drifted closed. Spence gathered her to his chest, and she lifted her arms to circle his neck. His tongue slid along her bottom lip, seeking entry, and she opened her mouth to him.

Never in Tricia's life had there been such a kiss. And never had she responded with such abandon, or had such overwhelming cravings for more. The heat from his hard, muscled body wove into hers, licking alive a trail of desire as it went.

She filled her senses with him. His aroma was heady and male; his hair was like silk beneath her fingers. Her breasts were crushed to his chest in a pleasant, exciting pain. His tongue dueled seductively with hers, and Tricia wondered absently if she was going to faint again.

Spence drank of Tricia's sweetness, relishing the feeling of her in his arms. He told himself to let her go, leave his hands on her arms, and then he gave up the battle. His hands moved to her slender throat, before sinking his fingers into her dark curls and bringing her mouth harder against his.

Blood pounded through his veins and his manhood stirred with the want and need of this lovely creature. His tongue mated with hers, imitating what his entire body ached to do. Somewhere in the deep recesses of his mind a voice screamed: What in hell are you doing?

He tore his mouth from hers. "Tricia," he said.

"Hmmm?" she asked dreamily, slowly opening her eyes.

"Oh, Lord, not that again." He took her by the shoulders and moved her away from him. "I'm sorry."

"You are?" she asked, her voice unsteady. "Oh, darn. I thought it was a wonderful kiss."

"It was."

"Really?" She smiled brightly. "On a scale of one to ten, how would you rate it?"

"An eleven," he said gruffly, "but it shouldn't have happened. I'm tired, I wasn't thinking clearly. Just forget it, okay?" Someone should tell his body to forget it. He was dying.

"No, I won't forget it," she said, picking up her tote bag. "It was marvelous. I'm putting it in 'my memories to keep.' "

"Your what?"

"I have this imaginary treasure chest in my heart. In there, I place special things, memories to keep. That's where that kiss is going. I really must be getting to my office. I'll see you later, Spence, when you come by to get the information you need."

She walked to the door, turned back to smile at him, then disappeared.

Spence took a deep breath, let it out, and ran his hand down his face, feeling the stubble of beard. Memories to keep, he repeated silently. *His* kiss? No joke? Was that corny? It should be corny, like a dewy-eyed teenage girl writing in her diary. But somehow, when Tricia had looked up at him with those big, dark eyes and told him about her treasure chest in her heart, it sounded so damn nice, so rare and special.

"Oh, forget it," he muttered. "I need some sleep, that's all. Tricia Todd is definitely not my type. Lord, is she for real?"

He shook his head and strode from the office. He mumbled his thanks to the secretary, then headed for the stairs. He was starving, he realized. He needed a shower, a shave, and some sleep. When he saw Tricia Todd again later that day he'd be able to view her as nothing more than an attractive, if somewhat flaky, woman. Fine.

Tricia inserted her key into the door and stepped into the office. *Her* office. Her glance fell on the lettering on the glass door before she closed it behind her. Patricia Todd. Certified Public Accountant.

The office was small. It consisted of one fairly good sized room and a bathroom. There was no separate area for a secretary, but then, she couldn't afford one anyway.

She had furnished the office in bright, cheerful colors. There was an orange filing cabinet next to a yellow one, and chairs of the same color faced the desk. Lush plants hung in the bank of windows, and an orange and brown tweed love seat stood against the wall.

She turned on the lights, flicked off her answering machine, whose steady red light indicated she had no messages, then walked over to the windows. The busy downtown area of Denver was spread out below her, and she could see the famous Brown Palace Hotel and the skyscrapers surrounding it, their upper floors hidden by low-hanging clouds. Her gaze swept over the Mile High City, but her thoughts were centered on Spence Walker.

Her fingertips came to rest on her lips as she replayed in her mind the kiss she had shared with Spence. Her senses still hummed from the sensual impact of his mouth on hers, of being held in his arms and pressed against his magnificent body. He had kissed her with obvious experience, his strength tempered with gentleness, with the touch of a man who knew women. He exuded a raw, blatant sexuality that was both exciting and frightening.

Spence was definitely out of her league.

"Oh, well," she said with a sigh. "At least I have one of my memories to keep."

She pulled her mind back to the present, retrieved a file from the yellow cabinet, then sat down behind her desk.

What a morning, she thought. She'd been trying to do nothing more than work on her physical fitness program when she'd been caught in the middle of a dramatic scenario of cops and robbers and guns. Things like that didn't happen to her. And men like Spence Walker didn't happen to her, either. Well, it was all over now. She was safe and sound in her cubbyhole office. Of course, Spence was going to drop by later, but that was strictly police business. Certainly there would be no more mind-boggling kisses.

She'd never responded to a kiss the way she had to Spence's, she mused. Then again, she'd never had guns pointed at her, or fainted into the arms of a man before. The entire episode was absurd. Better to tuck it into her treasure chest and forget it.

"Fine," she said, but once more her fingertips pressed against her lips.

The telephone rang suddenly and she jumped. She snatched up the receiver.

"Patricia Todd, CPA," she said cheerfully.

"Tricia, she's driving me nuts," a woman said.

"Hi, Kathy. What has our mother done now?"

"Beulah," Kathy said. "If the baby is a girl, she wants me to name her Beulah because it means 'she who will be married.' She said that maybe if she'd named you Beulah you wouldn't be an old maid. I can't stand much more of this."

Tricia laughed. "Kathy, humor her, agree to anything."

"Beulah? Over my dead body."

"I didn't say actually do it, just pretend you're going to. Oh, if Tony is looking for his squirt gun, it's in my tote bag."

"Half the world is in that tote bag. Do you suppose Patricia means, 'she who collects junk'?"

"Heavens, no. Mom said it means 'well-born, of the nobility.' "

"Really? Maybe there's a king in your future. Kathleen means 'pure,' you know. Pure? Me? How does Mother think I'm pregnant with my second child? There's something in the water? Tricia, I'm not going to survive her."

"Sure you will," Tricia said. "Go have a glass of milk. I've got to get to work."

"Well, okay. Have a good day, sweetie."

"It's been . . . interesting so far."

"Oh?"

"I'll tell you later. 'Bye." Beulah? Tricia mused after she'd hung up. That was definitely a bit much. What did the name Spencer mean? Oh, who cared? But it wouldn't surprise her at all if it meant 'he who kisses like a dream.' "Enough, Patricia. Add up some numbers."

"Spence?"

"Yeah?" Spence said, not looking up from the report he was working on.

"We got Freddy tucked away at Juvenile. His hearing is set for ten tomorrow morning."

Spence glanced up at the officer. "So soon?"

"They're overcrowded out there. I guess the latest fad is to be a junior hood."

"Wonderful," Spence muttered. He laced his fingers behind his head and leaned back in his chair. "I've never been involved in one of these before. Are there special forms to fill out?"

"No, just go with the regular set, and get a signed statement from the dingle-dangle darling that she agrees with *your* statement regarding her part in it."

Spence lunged forward, his palms landing with a smack on the desk. "What did you call her?"

The officer laughed. "Freddy was still blithering about the sexy cop who threatened to shoot him in the dingle-dangle. He is one shook-up kid, let me tell you. Anyway, everyone around here is getting a charge out of the story."

"It's nobody's damn business," Spence roared.

"You're sure in a terrific mood. Why don't you get some sleep? You look lousy."

"What? Oh, yeah, I'm going home in a few minutes."

"You'll be doing the world a favor," the officer said under his breath as he walked away.

"Well, hell," Spence said to the empty room. He slouched back in his chair again. "Freddy gave up, didn't he? So what if Tricia sounded a little flaky? It's nobody's damn business!"

"Talk to yourself much?" a woman in uniform asked from the doorway.

"That's enough. I've had it," Spence said, and stood up. "I'm getting out of this zoo. I need some sleep."

"Rest well, mighty Lieutenant," the woman said, batting her eyes at him. "From the top of your gorgeous head, all the way to your dingle—"

"Don't say it." He glared at her. "Don't even think it."

He strode through the crowded squad room and out the door, the sound of laughter trailing after him.

Just before five o'clock, Spence stepped out of the elevator on the fourth floor of the building Tricia worked in and went in search of her office. He was dressed in jeans, a pale blue shirt, and a lightweight Windbreaker to conceal the gun nestled in the back of his belt. He also wore a deep frown.

During his nap he'd dreamed of Tricia, and was none too happy about it. He never dreamed. He'd perfected the ability to blank his mind and simply sleep. Hell, the stuff he dealt with as a cop was bad enough without watching reruns of it in his sleep. But today he dreamed of Tricia.

He'd been holding her, carrying her through a field of wildflowers, and she'd been smiling at him. Corny. Really corny.

He stopped outside of Tricia's office and stared at her name on the glass door. He should never have kissed her, he told himself. Yeah, well, tired men often did weird things. But what a kiss it had been. No, forget it. Now rested, he'd walk through that door and see Tricia for what she was. An attractive, pleasant woman, who was definitely, *most definitely*, not his type. The kiss would be forgotten.

With a decisive nod he entered the office. Tricia looked up immediately, and smiled.

"Hello, Spence," she said. Oh, how long the day had been, waiting for this moment, she thought.

"Hello, Tricia," he said. You're in trouble, Walker, his little voice whispered. You're in deep, deep trouble.

Two

As Tricia watched Spence walk toward her, she was once again struck by his handsome, tanned face and vivid blue eyes. The wide set of his shoulders did not escape her, nor did the way his jeans hugged his hips and thighs. There was an athletic gracefulness to his walk, and, oh, she thought, what muscle tone.

A memory of the kiss they'd shared flashed through her mind, and a funny flutter danced along her spine.

"Nice place," he said, glancing around.

"It's small, but I'm proud of it. I opened this office six months ago, when I struck out on my own."

"Good for you." He wandered over to the windows. "Where'd you work before?"

"I was one of several bookkeepers for a large corporation. It was secure, but having my own company was my ultimate goal. So here I am."

She laughed. "If I don't starve to death, everything will be great. I'm getting clients slowly but surely."

Spence walked back to her desk and sat on its edge, keeping one foot on the floor. Tricia's eyes were riveted to the hard thigh directly in front of her.

"Did you have any aftereffects from this morning?" he asked.

The guns, no, she thought. The kiss? Now, that was a different ballgame. "No," she said, shifting her gaze from Spence's thigh to his face. "Do you jog?"

"When I have time."

"You have marvelous muscle tone."

"Muscle tone?" he asked, his eyebrows shooting up.

"Yes. Do you do other kinds of exercise to keep in shape?"

Spence frowned slightly and searched Tricia's face for any hint that she was being coy, making an innuendo about his preference of "exercise." He saw none. She was apparently asking a straightforward question, and was waiting for an answer.

"There's a gym at the police academy," he said. "I do whatever strikes my fancy when I get out there. Why?"

"Because I've embarked upon a physical fitness program," she said, "and I'm failing miserably. I hated jogging, and my first attempt at stair-climbing nearly got me shot. I can't decide what to try next."

"You look like you're in good shape," he said, his gaze sweeping over as much of her as he could see. Great shape, he thought. Perfect shape. She had molded to him as if she were custom ordered.

"Oh, I'm not fat," she said, "but I'm mushy."

He nearly choked. "You're what?" he asked, leaning toward her.

"Mushy, soft, no muscle tone."

"Oh, I see." He wasn't touching that one with a ten-foot pole. He could tell her how feminine she'd felt in his arms, curved in all the right places and soft, like heaven itself. Her breasts were firm and would nestle in the palms of his hands. The hell with muscle tone! "You could swim or ride a bike, I guess," he said, pushing himself off the desk.

She nodded thoughtfully. "Maybe."

Tricia Todd in a bikini, he thought. Lord. Or in skimpy little shorts for bike riding. Lord, Lord, Lord.

"I appreciate your suggestions," she said. "I figured that someone in your superb condition might know what I could do in the way of exercise."

Once more he looked at her for a sign of double meaning to her words, but found none. Was she for real? he wondered again. Apparently, she was. She was sweet, honest, and open. And he'd bet his pension she was a virgin. She was the furthest thing possible from the type of woman he preferred. And he found her absolutely enchanting.

"Yeah, well," he said, clearing his throat, "I need you to take a look at this report I'm turning in about Freddy. If it all seems in order to you, the events on the stairs described the way you remember them, there's a place for you to sign as a witness." He pulled some papers from the inside pocket of his Windbreaker and handed them to her.

"Of course," she said. " 'Frederick, aka Freddy, Jackson, age seventeen,' " she read aloud. "He's awfully young, isn't he? It seems a shame that he's chosen the wrong road for himself. He's hardly more than a boy."

"That *boy*," Spence said harshly, "is a sleazeball from the word *go*. He's mixed up with a pretty rough street gang. From the stuff Freddy's been involved in the past few weeks, I'd guess he's being initiated into the gang. He's been hauled in along with some others, but there was never enough evidence to make it stick. It's been penny-ante junk, more of a nuisance. Until now."

"Now?" she asked, frowning up at him.

"Now he's in real trouble, and we've got him cold. I'll just sit here while you read that." He settled onto the yellow chair and propped an ankle on his other knee.

"Maybe he has a bad home life," Tricia said.

"Who?"

"Freddy."

"Dammit, Tricia, don't do a bleeding-heart number for that scum."

"There's two sides to every story, Spence. Freddy wasn't born a scum. He was somebody's baby boy. He was cuddly and cute, took his first step, cut his first tooth. He started out the same way you did. Something happened to him along the way."

"Yeah, he turned into a slime," Spence said gruffly. "And I, for one, was not cute." He ran his hand over the back of his neck. "Let's get this over with. Just read the report, okay?"

"All babies are cute," she said. "There's no such

thing as a non-cute baby. Why would you say you weren't a cute baby?"

"Would you just read the damn report?" Spence said, and his voice seemed to bounce off the walls.

"Well, don't get huffy, Lieutenant. Personally, I think it's a very reasonable question. When one says one wasn't a cute baby, a person can't help but wonder why one would make that assessment. You know what I mean?"

"There is nothing cute," he said through clenched teeth, "about a bald, toothless wonder whose ears stick out. Satisfied? Fine. Read the report."

She laughed. "I bet you were adorable. And I must say, you produced marvelous hair and teeth once you got the hang of it. If your ears still stick out, no one will ever know."

"Thank you," he said dryly, staring at the ceiling as he strove for patience. "You can't believe what that does for my peace of mind."

"You're welcome. Now then." She snapped her wrists to straighten the papers. "Let's see what you have to say here about Freddy."

She wasn't for real, Spence told himself. No way. This was a setup. Ted had done this. He was pulling a practical joke on him, right? Wrong.

Spence rested his elbows on the arms of the chair and made a steeple of his fingers over the bridge of his nose. His gaze was focused on Tricia.

She was something, he thought, a slow smile tugging onto his lips. Whenever anything popped into her head, she just opened her mouth and said it. She'd actually got him talking about what he'd looked like as a baby, for Pete's sake. He'd seen his baby pictures. He'd been ugly as sin, although his mother had a conniption fit whenever he said that. Well, what did mothers know? They thought their offspring were terrific, no matter what.

Tricia would be a great mother, he thought. Her home would be filled with sunshine and that windchime laughter of hers. She'd flit around like a crazy little hummingbird, seeing to everyone's needs. Lucky baby. And lucky guy who came in the front door every night. She wasn't *his* type, of course, but he could picture her in a home with a husband and a baby. With a husband . . .

Spence frowned and shifted uncomfortably in his chair. He stared at Tricia, envisioning the shadowy figure of a man easing her onto a bed, then moving over her. That louse! he raged. Tricia was an innocent who deserved to be treated like a precious gem, like—

"Oh, for crying out loud," he said, smacking the arm of the chair with his hand. "This is ridiculous."

"I'm reading as fast as I can," Tricia said.

"Huh? Oh, take your time. Take all the time you need. Really. No rush. I was thinking about something else. Ignore me. Pretend I'm not here."

She eyed him warily, then buried her nose back in the papers.

You, Spence said to himself, are going to get shipped to the farm.

"Lieutenant," Tricia said.

"It's Spence."

"Spence. Don't you think this report is a bit harsh? You make such a whoop-de-do over the fact that Freddy was carrying a gun, then casually mention that it wasn't loaded. His weapon wasn't any more dangerous than mine. And yes, he threatened me, but I said I was going to shoot him in the—the place where I said I was going to shoot him. That's tit for tat. He didn't break into this building or steal anything. Now, I ask you, is that a hardened criminal? Certainly not. He's just a mischievous boy who—"

"Hold it!" Spence yelled. Tricia jumped. "Freddy Jackson, according to the evidence and our past experience in these matters, is being initiated into a street gang. By his own choosing, I might add. We received an anonymous tip that a slew of offices were going to be ripped off in this building last night; phone equipment, typewriters, the works. Apparently, part of Freddy's initiation is to see how well he can avoid being caught by the cops. He's a junior hoodlum on the road to the big time."

"Why?"

"What?"

"What is motivating his anger at society? What is his problem?"

"He has a screw loose. Would you just sign that thing and be done with it?"

She tapped the pen against her chin and cocked her head to one side. "I don't know if I can, in all good conscience."

"Oh," Spence moaned, "spare me."

"It says here that Freddy goes before the judge at juvenile court at ten tomorrow morning."

"Right," Spence said, smiling brightly. "Let's leave it to those who are in the know about these thugs . . . I mean, these troubled youths. Good idea? You bet. Sign the paper."

"Well," she said slowly, "I guess so."

"Great," he said as he got to his feet. He held his breath as Tricia's pen hovered just above the paper, then released it in a rush of air as she signed her name. "That'll do it," he said, snatching up the papers. Now he could leave, he thought. There was no reason for him to hang around. "Are you ready to quit for the day?" he asked.

"Yes."

"Would you like to get something to eat?" What? Where had that idea come from?

"Why?" she asked.

Why? he repeated silently. Wasn't anything simple with this woman? "Because I'm hungry," he said. "And it's the time of day when people have dinner. I just thought we could have a hamburger someplace."

"I'd be delighted," she said. She stood up and turned on her answering machine.

"You would?" he said. Hell, now she had *him* asking stupid questions. "Forget it. Let's go."

"Give me a minute to freshen up," she said, and carried her bag into the bathroom.

Spence was certainly moody, she thought as she brushed her hair. One minute he was chatty and pleasant, the next he was as crabby as all get out. And he was so intense too. Energy seemed to radiate from him, a wired readiness, as though he never totally relaxed. There was so much power in that body. What kind of lover was he?

"Shame on you," she whispered to her reflection in the mirror. Why had she agreed to have dinner with him? She had no business in the company of a man like Spence Walker, a man who had caused her to tremble when he'd taken her into his arms and kissed her. The men she dated were easygoing, calm, sedate. Almost boring, in fact, but that was all right. Her energies were directed toward establishing her business, so her social life took a very quiet back seat. Well, going out for a hamburger was no big deal. She'd just eat it and go home.

She stepped out of the bathroom and halted abruptly. Spence was standing in front of the windows, looking out, his hands shoved into the back pockets of his jeans. Her gaze swept over him and she swallowed heavily.

There was such sensual promise in every rugged inch of him, she thought. She was just so *aware* of him, of his strength, how he moved. And she was aware that each part of her body wonderfully complemented each part of his, and that there were such fascinating differences between men and women. It was exciting, but it was frightening.

"I'm ready, Spence," she said. Her voice was not quite steady.

He turned to face her and frowned instantly. Something was wrong, he thought. Tricia's eyes were wide and round and she had a stranglehold on that enormous bag of hers. Was she afraid of him? Damn, he didn't like that idea, not one little bit. Well, what did he expect? He'd hauled her into his arms and kissed her senseless this morning. Of course, she had kissed him back. But what did he know about dealing with innocents? Nothing. He felt old and jaded compared to her. He was thirty-five, going on a hundred.

He shook his head and crossed the room to her. She stared up at him.

"Look," he said, "I'm obviously making you nervous, but you have no reason to be frightened of me. I know I kissed you this morning, but that doesn't mean I'm about to jump your bones. We're just going to get something to eat."

"I have no idea what you're referring to," she said, hoping she sounded extremely huffy. "I'm not afraid of you, Spence Walker."

"No?" he said, smiling. "Well, that's comforting. So if I decided to kiss you right now, you wouldn't get the screaming meemies or faint all over me again."

"Of course I wouldn't," she said, fluffing her curls with one hand as she stared at a button on his shirt. Would she? Oh, help!

"Maybe," he said, his voice very, very low, "we should check this out." Don't do it, Walker, the little voice said. Don't kiss her.

"Oh, well, I don't think . . ."

He tilted her chin up with one finger. "Tricia."

That was all he said, just "Tricia," and she felt her knees turn to jelly. She met his gaze, and the tension emanating from him seemed to sweep through her in waves, leaving desire in its wake.

Spence slowly lowered his head to hers and he caught her soft sigh of consent with his mouth. Their bodies seemed to move of their own volition, seeking warmth, finding heated passion.

The kiss intensified. Hands roamed and breathing became labored. Hearts beat like pounding drums in an ever-quickening rhythm.

Tricia drifted in a mindless daze, not thinking,

only feeling. Her body hummed with sensuality and the essence of Spence. Their whole selves seemed to mingle, blending into one entity that was being consumed by nearly shattering pleasure.

Passion and need tightened within Spence, stirring his manhood with a gathering force. A shudder ripped through him, and he knew he was reaching the limit of his control. He had to stop. Now.

"Tricia," he said, his voice harsh, "no more."

Unable to speak, she nodded and stepped slowly, reluctantly, out of his embrace. He caught her hands and brought each to his mouth, gently kissing her palms. She trembled with desire.

"I'm very glad that you're not frightened of me," he said, "but, Tricia, don't . . . don't trust me too much. I'm a man, not a saint, and I want you. Lady, I don't think you have any idea how much I want you."

"I do trust you, Spence. You make me feel new, changed, as though I just arrived in my body and I'm discovering all the mysteries of it."

"Ah, Tricia." He placed a hand on her cheek. "Be careful. Be wary of me, of men like me. Your life is so different from mine, a life of treasure chests and memories to keep. You're special and rare, and you deserve love and commitment, marriage and babies."

"No, I'm not ready for those things. Even if my name were Beulah I wouldn't be ready. I'm concentrating on making a success of my business."

"Yeah, fine, but that doesn't erase the fact that you don't move in the fast lane. You live in a—who's Beulah?"

Tricia laughed, at last breaking the sensual spell that had hung heavily in the air.

"Buy me a hamburger and I'll tell you all about Beulah," she said, smiling up at him.

He matched her smile. "You're on."

Out in the corridor, Tricia locked the door, but Spence reached around her and rattled the knob. He thumped the heel of his hand against the wood surrounding the glass, then ran his fingers down the glass panel.

"Junk," he said. "Loose tumblers, flimsy wood, no wire in the glass. It's hardly worth locking the door. If Freddy had really intended to help himself to what you own, it would have been a cinch to get in there."

"But that *wasn't* his intention. He was—was playing hide-and-seek."

"Oh, good Lord," Spence said, rolling his eyes. "Now I've heard everything."

"Well, he was. You know, now that I think about it, Freddy is a nice-looking young man. Cut that shaggy hair of his, scrub him up a little, and he'd be real cute. He's got eyelashes most girls would kill for."

"Tricia, are you telling me that in the middle of that chaos, during which you threatened to shoot Freddy in the dingle-dangle, you noticed his eyelashes?"

She shrugged. "Guess so. Isn't it amazing what one's subconscious retains? Fascinating. Spence, why do you yell so much?"

"I don't yell!" he yelled.

"Mmm," she said skeptically, and started down the hall. Spence muttered an earthly expletive, then fell in step beside her.

The July night was warm but not oppressive. The first rosy glow of the sunset was settling over the city as they walked through the parking lot at the rear of the building. They agreed to go in Spence's car, then he would bring her back to get hers after dinner.

Tricia watched Spence as he drove, watched the intriguing play of his muscled thighs beneath the soft fabric of his jeans as he pressed the pedals, the firm but relaxed grip of his large hands on the steering wheel.

At first glance he appeared at ease, but he wasn't. It was always there, that coiled readiness, that underlying power just waiting to break loose. What a man, she thought. He was like none she had ever met before.

The restaurant that he selected was homey rather than fancy, and the waitresses were wearing ging-ham dresses. They were shown to a booth and both ordered hamburgers with French fries.

"I'm surprised you don't have a full meal packed away in that tote bag," Spence said.

"I *did*," Tricia said. "My lunch."

He laughed. "Now, who is Beulah?"

"Actually, no one. When my older sister, Kathy, was expecting her first baby, my mother took up the hobby of researching what names mean. Thing is, she never quit doing it. Kathy is pregnant again and in no mood for our mother's nonsense. Beulah means 'she who will be married,' and Mother thinks that's a splendid name for a girl."

"Your mother is all for girls being married, I take it?"

"Oh, yes. I turned twenty-five last month and

she cried when I blew out the candles on my cake. Poor me." She laughed. "I'm officially an old maid now."

"You don't seem too worried about it," Spence said.

"Like I said before, I'm concentrating on getting my business established. I want to marry someday, and have three or four children."

"Four?"

"Well, I'd be willing to compromise and have two. Do you have brothers or sisters?"

"No."

"Are your parents here in Denver?"

"Yes. My father is a retired cop. My folks have been married for nearly forty years."

"That's an impressive record in today's society. Have you ever been married?"

"How do you know I'm not?"

"You don't act married," she said, shrugging.

"You're so trusting, it's a crime. But, no, I've never been married."

"Why?"

"Do you have a sentimental attachment to that word?" he asked, grinning at her. "Okay. I've never gotten married because I haven't found anyone I wanted to spend the rest of my life with."

"The translation of which is, you're a bed-hopper."

"That's a crummy thing to say, Tricia!"

"Don't you start yelling again, Spence Walker," she said, glaring at him. "I was simply chatting."

"I'm not a bed-hopper," he said in a loud whisper, leaning toward her. "I'm—I'm a normal, healthy man, that's all."

"I rest my case," she said, smiling sweetly.

"Knock it off." He slouched back against the booth. "Look, I'm cautious, all right? A lot of women aren't prepared for the life of being a cop's wife. The divorce rate is extremely high."

"Because of the danger, I suppose."

"And the long hours, the fact that you can't always be home when you said you would. But, yes, I'd say mainly because the wife doesn't know when her husband leaves if he'll come back."

"Does any wife?" Tricia asked. "Not really. My father worked in a bank. He left the house, went to his office, sat down at his desk, and had a heart attack. He died instantly. I was fifteen."

"That's rough."

"The point is, there are no guarantees about anything. I'd rather take an optimistic view and have hopes and dreams. If I were married to a police officer, I wouldn't stop planning for the tomorrows I would share with that man. Goodness, that would be a terribly gloomy way to live."

Spence frowned. "Cops are never really off duty, Tricia. I'm wearing a gun right now."

"Well," she said, winking at him, "don't worry about a thing, partner, because my trusty squirt gun is right here in my tote bag. I'll be ready if you need me."

An expression of surprise crossed his face, then he laughed. Again the question niggled in his mind: Was Tricia Todd for real?

"Plates are hot, folks," the waitress said, setting their dinners down on the table. "I'll be right back with your drinks."

Tricia spread her napkin across her lap. "This looks delicious."

"It's just a hamburger," Spence said.

"But I think this is a homemade bun." She bit into the burger. "Definitely homemade. Isn't that marvelous?"

Spence took a large bite of his own hamburger. Now she was all charged up over hamburger buns? he thought incredulously. Sure, it tasted good, but he'd eaten here a hundred times and never paid any attention to the buns. Why was he wasting his brain space thinking about hamburger buns? Jeez.

The waitress returned to their table. "Here are your drinks."

"Are these buns homemade?" Tricia asked.

"You bet, honey. The specialty of the house. Keeps folks coming back time after time."

Spence halted his hamburger halfway to his mouth and stared at it as if he'd never seen one before in his life.

When they were through eating, Spence asked Tricia why she'd decided to become an accountant.

"I love math," she answered. "It's so stable, you know what I mean? Two plus two is always four. I'm actually not a very organized person. I make lists of things I need to do, then lose the lists. I carry this tote bag because there's a fighting chance that what I need is in there. Somewhere in this town is a cleaners holding a jacket of mine for ransom, but for the life of me I can't remember where it is."

He laughed.

"But math?" she continued. "Those little numbers, bless their hearts, always do what they're supposed to do. I do profit and loss statements for businesses, income tax returns for individuals, the works. It's the only aspect of my life that has any semblance of order. I think my brain shifted or something and sent all my organization signals to that one area. I'm a terrific accountant and a lousy everything else." She shrugged. "Oh, well."

"I bet you're not all that bad at everything else."

"If you knew how many times I've run out of gas, you'd agree with me. I've decided to accept myself the way I am. Except for my body, of course. I'm definitely going to keep after my physical fitness program."

"Muscle tone."

"Exactly."

"Well, just remember to start out easy, building up your exercise time slowly, or your muscles will be screaming for mercy. Would you like some dessert? They have great pie here."

"Do you suppose it's homemade?"

He shook his head in resignation. "I have no idea."

The waitress enthusiastically informed them that the pie was indeed homemade and Tricia beamed. Spence frowned. He didn't know why he was irritated, but it bothered him for some insane reason that Tricia had discovered the uniqueness of the food here and was finding such pleasure in it. When he'd eaten in this restaurant in the past, he'd just stuffed his face and gone about his business. Why was he making a big deal out of such a trivial matter anyhow? He should just forget it.

"You're rather moody, aren't you?" Tricia asked as they ate their pie.

"What?" he said. "Moody? Me?"

"It wasn't a criticism, just an observation. You switch moods very quickly."

"No, I don't." He frowned. "Do I?"

"Well, it's extremely understandable. I imagine that in your line of work you have a great deal on your mind."

"I'm not moody," he said a trifle too loudly.

"Okay, cancel moody. How about 'intense'? Nope. You're still frowning. Do you like 'deep'?"

"Would you knock it off? I feel like I'm under a microscope."

"Sorry," she said pleasantly. "You're probably used to women who get so caught up with your gorgeous body, they don't look further."

"Tricia, for crying out loud," he said, glancing quickly at the nearby tables, "could we change the subject?"

"Why?"

"Because this conversation is nuts. Eat your pie."

"You don't like people getting too close to you, do you? Oh, I'm sure you enjoy your fair share of women who are . . . you know, close. But I'm referring to you the person, the man, who you really are."

"What are you? An amateur shrink?"

"No, I'm simply a woman who feels that people deserve to be appreciated for more than just their surface appearance. I didn't mean to offend you, Spence. I have a tendency to rattle on, say whatever is on my mind. I'm sorry." Darn, she thought miserably, she'd done it again. Why didn't she stop and think before she blithered on and on? Spence was obviously very annoyed with her. If she had a quarter for every time her big mouth had gotten her into trouble, she could go on a world cruise. "I really do apologize."

He looked at her for a long moment, then shook his head.

"No," he said, "don't apologize. You're one of the most open, honest, refreshing women I've ever met." And vulnerable, he added silently. The kind of woman that brought out a man's protective instincts. He had the strangest urge to stand between her and anything or anyone that could hurt her. "I shouldn't have snapped at you. You just caught me by surprise, that's all. The women I . . . Well, never mind."

"I know," she said, sighing. "They're sophisticated, say all the right things at the right times."

Yeah, he thought dryly, like "You're a terrific lover, Spence. Call me the next time you want to go to bed." Hell, the women he knew didn't care what mood he was in as long as they had their fun. What a crummy picture it all painted in his mind. He *was* a bed-hopper. He'd just never thought about it before. Thanks to Miss Chattercheeks Todd, he was becoming thoroughly depressed.

"I think I'd better be getting home," Tricia said quietly.

"Hey, wait a minute," he said, covering her hand with his. "I'm the one apologizing. There was no reason for me to bite your head off. I'm giving you the impression that you did something wrong. Being interested in who a person really is isn't wrong. With the people I know, it's unusual, that's all. I'm not used to anyone wanting to get close to me in the sense you mean."

"And you hate it."

"I'll have to give it some thought," he said, smiling. "You must be tired. You've had a wild day." He signaled to the waitress. "I'll take you back to your car, then follow you home so I know you got there safely."

"That isn't necessary."

"Humor me. I assume you live alone?"

"Yes."

"In an apartment with a security guard?"

"No, I have a cute little cottage at the end of a quiet street. I'm next to a beautiful stretch of woods. It's like being in the country."

Logical, Spence thought wryly. Little Red Riding Hood just waiting for the Big Bad Wolf.

In the parking lot of Tricia's office building, Spence opened the car door for her, then leaned over to check the gas gauge after she'd turned on the ignition.

"Half a tank," he said. "Not bad. I'll follow you."

"I'll probably do ten things wrong because I'm being followed by a policeman."

"Just forget I'm there."

Forget Spence Walker was there? Tricia mused as she pulled out onto the road. Not a chance. He was there when he wasn't there, for he'd stayed in her mind the entire day. Her heart had started racing the moment he'd entered her office. But, darn it, the differences between their worlds were so glaringly obvious. She didn't have one iota of sophistication. She didn't know how to impress a man like Spence.

So what? she asked herself. She knew he was out of her league, was one of the untouchables she occasionally glanced at from afar. Men like Spence weren't hers to have. So why was she suddenly feeling so sorry for herself?

The kisses. The kisses she'd shared with Spence, the wondrous sensations he'd created within her.

That was why she was sad, she realized. She'd had a fleeting glimpse of the woman within her, who had been brought alive by the touch of a magnificent man. Spence had taken her to a place she had never been to before. And, oh, she liked it there, with Spence, but knew she couldn't stay. She would only have memories to keep.

"Darn it," she said. "No. Dammit. This definitely calls for dammit."

She pulled into her driveway and turned off the ignition. Spence stopped right behind her, swung out of his car, and strode toward her with heavy steps.

"Uh-oh," she muttered. "Now what did I do?" She got out of the car and smiled weakly.

"Have you ever heard of turn signals?" he asked, towering over her, his hands planted on his hips.

"Of course. I used them at every corner."

Spence shook his head, slid behind the wheel of her car, and turned the key in the ignition.

"Go to the rear and tell me what you see," he said.

"I know what a turn signal looks like, Lieutenant," she said, stomping to the back of her car. "So, put it on."

"The left one is on!"

"It is not."

"Now the right," he said.

"Nope. Are you flicking that little stick thing?"

Spence swore and stepped out of the car.

"Miss Todd," he said tersely, "both of those light bulbs are burned out. I should write up a ticket for you."

"Oh, is that so? Well, answer me this. How am I supposed to know what's going on back here when I'm sitting up there? They're blinking inside, if you'll notice. Write your dumb ticket, I don't care. But I'll fight you all the way to the Supreme Court. I'll . . . I'll . . ."

"Shoot me in the dingle-dangle?" he asked, and burst into laughter. "Go ahead. Day my make."

"Don't you dare laugh at me," she yelled.

"Hey, I'm sorry." He pulled her into his arms. He was still smiling, and she glared up at him. "You've got a real hot temper when you get going," he said. "You're a scary lady."

"That's right, buster," she said. "I'm mean, lean, and tough. And mushy. No muscle tone. I'm working on that, though."

"I think we need to have an indepth discussion," he said, slowly lowering his lips toward hers, "regarding your muscle tone."

"Why?"

"Shh, I'm kissing you."

That was putting it mildly, Tricia thought dreamily as his mouth captured hers.

Any other thoughts she might have had disappeared into a hazy mist of sensuality as desire tingled through her. Spence's tongue delved deep into her mouth and she welcomed its intrusion. She slid her hands up his chest and inside his jacket to splay on his back, relishing the feel of his hard muscles.

Sweet, sweet, sweet, Spence thought as he explored each hidden crevice of Tricia's mouth. But it wasn't enough. He wanted more. He wanted all of her. He wanted her naked in his arms, nestled beneath him, and he would fill her with all he had to offer her. Gently, reverently, he would teach her the mysteries of her body and his, guide her on a sexual journey, and bring her safely back. *He* would be the one . . . to take her innocence?

"Damn," he said, jerking his head up.

"What?" Tricia asked. She blinked several times.

"You're a virgin, right?" he said, frowning as he gripped her shoulders. "Right? I'd make book on it. Well?"

"You're disgusting." She brushed his arms away. "Absolutely disgusting. Get out of my driveway. Get out of my life!" She marched around him, snatched her tote bag from the car, slammed the door shut, and started toward the house.

"Walker, you're nauseating," Spence muttered, staring up at the sky. "You made it sound like she has a disease. Ah, hell!" He spun around. "Tricia, wait."

"No!"

He sprinted after her and caught up with her just as she inserted her key in the door.

"It's open," she said as the door moved inward. "I know I locked it."

Spence pulled his gun from the back of his belt. "Stay here, Tricia. Don't come in until I call you."

"But—"

"Do it! Move away from the door."

Tricia scurried out of the way, then pressed her hands to her cheeks as Spence entered the dark house. Seconds ticked into minutes, and the sound of her heartbeat roared in her ears. She jumped when the lights came on inside, but still Spence did not reappear.

"Spence?" she said in a loud whisper. "Are you all right? Spence?"

He stepped out onto the porch and shoved the gun back into his belt. A deep frown knitted his tawny brows together.

"I'm sorry, Tricia," he said quietly. "Your house has been vandalized. It's a real mess. I called it in. I'm so damn sorry."

"I don't understand," she said, her voice trembling. "Who did this?"

"Kids, two boys high on drugs. They hit your place and two others close to here. The cops got them in the third house. They're fifteen years old."

"I see," she said softly, her eyes brimming with tears. "That's awfully young, isn't it? I really wish . . . they hadn't . . . done this."

"Ah, Tricia." He pulled her into his arms. "I'm here. I'm right here, and nothing bad is going to happen to you. I swear it."

Three

When Spence's teeth began to ache, he realized how tightly he was clenching his jaw. A hot fury surged through him, causing the pulse to beat wildly in his neck. He felt Tricia tremble in his arms, and forced himself to push aside his anger before he attempted to speak to her.

"Tricia," he said, striving desperately for a gentle tone, "I have to take you inside now. I need to know if anything has been taken. I'll be right there with you."

"Yes. Yes, all right," she said, and swallowed heavily.

He circled her shoulders with his arm and pulled her close to his side. She looked up at him with tears shimmering in her big dark eyes, and he felt as though a knife were twisting in his gut. His instincts told him to pick her up, carry her away from there, protect her from seeing the horror beyond the door. But as a police officer he had to follow procedure, take her inside, have her determine if anything had been stolen.

But one thing was for damn sure, he thought fiercely. Tricia wasn't going to have to handle this alone. He was right there beside her, and he wasn't budging.

His head snapped up as a patrol car stopped in front of the house. A dark sedan pulled up behind it. Two uniformed police officers emerged from the patrol car, and a man dressed in jeans and a cotton shirt got out of the sedan. The plainclothesman was Ted Baker, a detective on the force. He was six feet tall and tightly muscled. His hair was an unruly crop of dark brown waves, and his face had a boyish quality. He was married and had a year-old daughter. He and Spence had worked together on many occasions and trusted each other with their lives. They shared a solid friendship and mutual respect, which led to easy bantering between them. The three men strode to the porch, where Spence stood with Tricia.

"Ted," Spence said, nodding at his friend.

"I heard your call come in, Spence. I thought I'd come see if I could help."

"Thanks," Spence said. "Tricia Todd, meet Ted Baker. He's a lousy detective but basically a nice guy. Ted, Tricia Todd."

"Hello," Tricia said.

"Ma'am," Ted said. "Sorry you've had trouble here. Spence is a dud, but now that I'm on the scene everything is under control." Spence made a noise that could be described only as a snort.

"Lieutenants?" one of the uniformed officers said.

"Sit tight," Spence said. "Miss Todd hasn't been inside yet. I'll call you when we need you." He turned to Tricia. "Are you ready to go inside?"

"I guess so."

Spence and Ted exchanged a long look, then Spence led Tricia through the door. Ted followed behind them. Tricia stumbled slightly and Spence tightened his hold on her shoulders.

"Oh, God," she whispered.

It was a nightmare. Everywhere that her horrified gaze swept she saw destruction. The floor was strewn with books that had been pulled from the bookcases. The cushions from her white wicker furniture were flung in all directions. Figurines were broken, and her hanging plants had been smashed onto the carpeted floor.

Spence slowly moved Tricia forward. She was clutching her tote bag so tightly to her breasts that her knuckles were white.

"Your TV is here," he said quietly. "Do you own a stereo?"

"No."

"Any valuable jewelry, antiques?"

"No," she said, her voice quivering. "I don't have anything fancy. Just things I like. My books and plants. Oh, Spence, my beautiful plants are ruined. I talked to them, you know, my plants. It's silly, I guess, but they were growing, and the leaves were shiny, and . . ."

"Shh. It's okay. Are you sure you didn't own anything of value? Say, a ring or watch that belonged to a grandparent, or a special painting? Anything?"

"No."

"All right." He gently pushed her into a chair. "You stay there for a minute. I have to talk to Ted and the other officers. Don't move, just sit."

She nodded. Her gaze once again roamed around the room, and she shivered. Spence looked at Ted and jerked his head indicating the kitchen. Ted followed him into the small room. Ted swore under his breath as he stepped over the debris that had been flung from the open cupboards onto the floor.

"And the bedroom?" he asked.

"The same," Spence said.

"She hasn't checked the other rooms for missing items."

"I don't want her seeing any more than she has to yet. She doesn't own anything worth taking except the TV."

"Well, she should do a walk-through."

"No," Spence snapped.

"Okay, buddy, no problem," Ted said, raising his hands.

"At least we've got those punks picked up," Spence said in a low voice. "Lord, Tricia's had a helluva day. First Freddy, now this." He took a deep breath and let it out slowly as he stared at the ceiling. He ran his hand down his face, then looked at Ted again. "I can't leave her here alone tonight, Ted."

"I know. She looks scared to death. Well, you'll take care of your lady."

"She's not my lady."

"I won't argue the point," Ted said, grinning, "since you're in the mood to bust somebody's jaw. All I know is that I just saw a gentle side to you, my boy, that I didn't know existed. I could have sworn you had ice water in your veins. Tricia Todd is defrosting you, Walker."

"Go to hell, Baker," Spence said, and added a colorful expletive.

Ted laughed. "Oh, I love it. Spence Walker is teetering on the edge of big-time heart trouble. Well, I'm off to scum city to see who else is up to no good. Where can I reach you?"

"Here or at home."

"Got it. Take tender lovin' care of Tricia, Spence. She looks like a frightened fawn. I'll send the uniforms in and check with you later."

Tricia was sitting ramrod stiff in the chair and jumped when Ted came out of the kitchen. He gave her a wide smile and a thumbs-up sign, then strode out the front door. Spence appeared and met the officers as they entered the house. They spoke in low voices, and Tricia gave up trying to hear what they were saying. She was having enough trouble trying not to cry.

Her beautiful little cottage, she thought miserably. Her plants were ruined, all her lovely plants. Why had those boys done such a vicious thing to her? Well, it wasn't personal, she supposed, but still . . .

She set her bag on the floor and stood up. She picked up several books and crossed the room to the bookcase.

"What are you doing?" Spence asked, walking up behind her as she carefully set the books on a shelf.

"Cleaning up this disaster." She turned to look at him. "I'm so disorganized, I'll probably find some things I didn't remember I had. How did those boys get in here?"

"The kitchen window. You don't have to start on this tonight."

"It isn't going to do itself." She picked up several more books. "Did those policemen leave?"

"Yeah," he said, and bent to pick up the sofa cushions. "Are you sure you want to do this tonight?"

"Yes."

"Would you like to call your family?"

"No, they'll just get upset. They didn't like this place when I chose it because it was so isolated. I'd never hear the end of it if they found out about this. Of course, they'd have a screaming fit if they knew I'd pointed a squirt gun at Freddy and threatened to shoot him. That was a dumb thing to do."

"It was extremely brave and innovative," Spence said, smiling at her. He scooped up an armload of books. "Here. Put these on the shelf. You can always arrange them in order later."

"I don't have any order for my books. That's what I hate about libraries. You have to whisper and worry about proper order on the shelves. I appreciate your help, Spence, but you don't have to stay. I'll just keep at it until I'm finished."

"Tricia," he said gruffly, "I'm not leaving you. I think you should let me get you settled into a hotel for the night."

"No."

"The day you've had is going to catch up with you. Why don't you put all of this on hold for now and tackle it in the morning?"

"I'll be busy in the morning."

"Hey, you're the boss of your business. You can't fire yourself. Take the morning off."

"I'll . . . um, think about it. In the meantime, I want to clean this up."

He sighed. "Okay, I won't argue with you. I'll keep my mouth shut and be an extra pair of hands."

"Thank you, Spence," she said quietly.

Their eyes met and held for a long moment. Spence was the first to break the contact, clearing his throat and reaching for more books. They worked in silence for the next ten minutes, Spence putting three books on the shelves to Tricia's one. He set the lamps back on the end tables, then picked up the broken pieces of ceramic.

"This room is in pretty good shape except for the plants," he said finally. "Do you have a big trash bag?"

"Under the kitchen sink. Spence, I think I should warn you that I'm about to cry. I mean, I postponed it for as long as I could but . . . I really need to cry, so if you'd like to go home, I'll understand because I'm a noisy crier."

"Tricia," he said. He crossed the room and pulled her into his arms. "You have every right to cry. Every right."

So she cried.

Spence sat down with her on the sofa and held her tightly. She clutched his jacket, buried her face in his shirt, and wept as though her heart were breaking. He pressed his hand to her head, weaving his fingers through her silky curls, and scowled.

He felt so damn helpless. He saw people cry all

the time in his line of work, but never had tears torn at him like Tricia's did. She sounded so sad, so scared. And she felt fragile and tiny in his arms, like a bird. She didn't deserve this hassle. She should be protected, cherished. Not by him, of course, but she needed a strong man in her life to watch over her.

What man? he wondered in the next instant. There were scums out there who would take advantage of an innocent like Tricia. He didn't like the idea of some other guy touching her, kissing her, holding her. What had Ted said? That Spence had heart trouble? No way. He wasn't getting emotionally involved with Tricia Todd.

So, okay, he was feeling very protective toward her at the moment. He was the one who had chased Freddy down those stairs and into Tricia's lap. And, yes, kissing her was heaven, and she felt sensational in his arms, but it wasn't enough to make a federal case out of. He'd see her through this mess, then say good-bye. Tricia was not his type.

She sniffled. He reached into his back pocket for a handkerchief.

"Thank you," she mumbled. "Your shirt is soggy."

"It'll dry. Pretend I'm not here. Cry for as long as you like."

"Ohh," she moaned. "Don't be so nice to me. Say something rude, then I'll get mad and quit crying."

He chuckled and her head bounced on his chest. She drew in a wobbly breath and slowly sat up, dabbing at her nose with the handkerchief.

"That's it?" he asked. "Wasn't much of a show. Feel free to continue."

"No, that's enough," she said, brushing tears from her cheeks. "If I cry anymore, I'll plug up my sinus cavities and get a rotten headache."

He grinned and shook his head. "That's your quota, huh? One soggy shirtfront. Hardly seems worth the effort."

"Oh, I feel much better. Well, I'd better get back to work. I'll be glad to wash your shirt and hankie."

"Don't worry about it. Look, I'll deal with those plants. And Tricia, the kitchen and bedroom are torn up too. I just wanted to warn you before you see them."

"Oh. Well, those boys certainly were organized. If I'd set out to do this, I'd probably forget to mess up one entire room."

Spence cradled her face in his hands and smiled at her warmly.

"You're really something," he said. One small kiss, he told himself. Just one. "A very special lady," he added, then covered her lips with his.

The kiss was so soft and tender, so gentle that fresh tears sprang to Tricia's eyes. She slid her hands up Spence's soggy shirt and around his neck, urging his mouth harder onto hers. She could feel his restraint, the rigid control that was causing his muscles to tremble.

No, she thought. She wanted him to kiss her, really kiss her and blot out the horror of the violation of her precious cottage, allowing her just to feel.

With a sense of daring mingled with desperation, she thrust her tongue into his mouth. He stiffened, groaning at this sweet intimacy, then dropped his arms to encircle her waist and crushed her body to his. He met her tongue with his and their passions soared.

Yes! Tricia thought.

No! Spence thought.

She pressed against him and, cursing himself, he gave up the battle.

He lifted his legs onto the sofa and leaned back, moving Tricia to lie on top of him. He drank in the taste, the feel of her as his mouth ravished hers. She answered in kind, kissing him urgently, a soft moan catching in her throat.

She could feel his arousal beneath her and savored the realization that a man like Spence Walker wanted her. Her. His large, strong hands were igniting flames of desire throughout her, and his potent kiss seemed to be carrying her away from reality.

He cupped her head in his hands and lifted her lips from his. Blood pounded through his veins and he ached with the want of Tricia.

"I want you," he said hoarsely. "No, don't say anything," he added as she started to speak. He pressed her head to his shoulder. "Just be still a minute. Don't move."

"But . . ."

"You're safe with me. I won't hurt you, Tricia. I need to cool off. Don't move."

She drew in a deep breath. Spence groaned.

"Sorry," she said. "I didn't move, I breathed."

"That's allowed," he said, chuckling softly. "Lord, you feel good. I didn't mean to get so carried away. I started kissing you, and I couldn't stop. You have a powerful effect on me, Miss Todd."

"I've never felt this way before, Spence. When you kiss me . . . I don't know. This is all so different, so new. I guess it's obvious I've never been with a man. I shouldn't have gotten so angry when you asked me if I was a virgin."

"I wasn't very polite about it. You're a special woman, and I made you sound like a social outcast or something. I'm sorry for the way I handled that. I think part of it was frustration from knowing I can't have you, can't make love with you. I do want you, Tricia, but I know it isn't going to happen."

She raised her head to look at him. "Why isn't it?" she asked.

"Don't be dense," he said, lifting her off him. As he sat up, he shrugged out of his jacket, then readjusted his gun in his belt.

"Try confused," she said.

"Tricia, I'm very aware of the fact that twenty-five-year-old virgins are an endangered species." She laughed. "This isn't funny!" he said. "If you were cut out for an affair, you would have had one by now. But you're waiting for everything—commitment, marriage, kids, the PTA."

"The PTA?"

"Yeah, the whole nine yards. I have nothing against marriage. I want to be married someday, have a family. But in the meantime, I have a different lifestyle from yours. I don't promise women anything. We understand each other. Going to bed with someone doesn't represent a lifelong commitment."

"You love 'em and leave 'em," she said dramatically, covering her heart with her hand.

"Yeah, sort of. Why do I get the feeling you're not taking what I'm saying seriously?"

"I am! I'm listening to every word. You're the kind of man my mother warned me to stay away from."

"I'm not *that* bad. Well, maybe I am."

"The thing is, Spence, you've read me wrong. Yes, I want to marry, but I'm not saving myself for that. I'm a virgin simply because I haven't found anyone I particularly wanted to make love with. Besides, I've been very busy. My innocence is a fluke, not a statement."

"Nope, I don't buy it."

"It's true."

"Tricia, I'm a cop. I'm trained to size up people very quickly because my life can depend on it. I sensed a difference, a lovely, unique difference in you when we met. Don't do it to yourself. Don't give your innocence to a man who isn't prepared to offer you what you deserve to have."

"That, Lieutenant Walker," she said, lifting her chin, "is my decision to make."

"Fine. Great." He stood up and shot her a stormy glare. "Have a wonderful time. Sleep with whoever strikes your fancy, but it isn't going to be me. I don't want you on my conscience! Because I'm telling you, Miss Todd, you'll be making a big mistake."

"Says you."

"Damn right. Come on, let's get this place cleaned up."

Before Tricia could think of a snappy reply, the telephone rang. Spence snatched up the receiver.

"Walker."

"What if that's my mother?" Tricia asked. He ignored her.

"Yeah, Ted," he said, then ran his hand over the back of his neck. "Okay . . . okay. I will. Thanks."

"Is something wrong?" Tricia asked as he hung up.

"Not really. Ted just called to see how you were doing and to say that the boy's parents picked them up. They'll be scheduled for a hearing at Juvenile."

"Maybe they'll meet Freddy," Tricia said.

Spence frowned. "This should erase any 'poor Freddy' thoughts from your mind. You've been the victim of two more kids who are on the same self-destructive road that he's on."

"Yes," she said, "but do they have gorgeous eyelashes?"

He smiled in spite of himself. "You are ba-nan-as." And fascinating, and beautiful, and he wanted her. Lord, how he wanted to make love to this woman. But, dammit, no matter what she said, she belonged to the man she would marry. Tricia Todd was not his to have. His brain knew that. It was his body that was slipping over the edge. "I'll get a trash bag and clean up the plants," he said, starting toward the kitchen.

She got to her feet and followed him, then gasped when she saw the destruction in the bright yellow room.

"Oh, Spence."

"It's grim. Be careful of the glass. I'll help you as soon as I finish the living room. Do you have a vacuum cleaner?"

"In the front closet. Those rats! They broke all my catsup. I got four bottles of catsup on sale, and they broke them. Those crumbs. I had to make four trips inside that store because it was one to a customer."

"You cheated the grocery store?" he asked in mock horror. "I'm surprised at you."

"I'm full of surprises," she said, wiggling her eyebrows.

He chuckled, then pulled a trash bag from the box on the floor and returned to the living room.

Full of surprises, Tricia mused as she began to replace cans in the cupboard. That was for sure. She'd surprised herself when she'd told Spence that she hadn't been particularly saving herself for the man she intended to marry. She hadn't really thought about it much, except she did know she had never wanted to sleep with any men she'd ever met. No man had set her aflame with a passion that consumed her senses.

Until Spence. Oh, yes, she did want Spencer Walker.

Hold it, she told herself as she tossed debris into the trash can. She was forgetting that Lieutenant Walker had stated adamantly that he had no intention of making love with her, even though he wanted her. He'd said as much, and besides, she'd been lying on top of his body and could swear under oath that he wanted her. But he was determined not to do a darned thing about it.

The sound of the vacuum cleaner brought her

from her tangled thoughts, and she welcomed the reprieve. She had been through enough for one day. A few minutes later Spence walked into the kitchen.

"The living room is done," he said.

"Thank you so much. I really appreciate—"

"Shh." He pulled his gun from his belt. "Go into the living room."

"Why?"

"Don't you ever get tired of asking that? There's someone outside the kitchen door. Go!"

She cocked her head in the direction of the door. "That's the cat."

"You didn't mention you had a cat."

"I don't. He thinks he's mine, but he isn't."

Spence flung open the door and a huge black cat strolled in, meowing loudly.

"Hello, Cat," Tricia said. "Hungry? We're having a special on catsup."

"You feed it? No wonder it thinks it lives here." Spence glanced around outside before shutting the door, then replaced his gun in his belt. "That's an ugly cat, Tricia."

"I know, but he has personality. Somewhere in this mess is a packet of food for him."

"If you quit feeding him, he'd stop coming around."

"But then I'd worry that he was going hungry. Here it is." She pulled a small package from beneath a roll of paper towels. "His bowl is on the back porch."

"I'll do it. You stay in here. Come on, Ugly."

"His name is Cat."

"That's very original."

Outside, Spence dumped the food into the bowl. The cat gave him a rather bored stare and began to eat.

Why couldn't Tricia live in a high-rise apartment building? Spence mused as he scanned the heavily wooded area beyond the cottage. Night was falling quickly, and her house seemed even more isolated. She was lucky she hadn't had trouble before now. She had no business living out here like this. Lord, she was enough to give a cop an ulcer. And enough to give a man a constant ache in his loins.

Why did he want her so much? he asked himself. Was it some kind of mind game, his wanting what he couldn't have? No, he didn't think so. He had been turned down before and had simply shrugged it off, not really caring. The situation with Tricia was different, but the result was the same: He couldn't have her. And he wanted her like no woman before.

He sighed, a deep, weary sigh that seemed to come from the very depths of his soul. A breeze rustled the leaves on the trees in the woods, and to Spence the sound was lonely and forlorn. But Tricia, he knew, would hear it as a lovely melody sung by nature just for her. Oh, she was something, all right. She was innocence, fresh air, and sunshine. When he moved on down the road, she would be one of his memories to keep.

"Spence?"

He turned around and saw her standing in the doorway. "Yes?"

"I'm going to wash the kitchen floor. Use the front door when you come in, okay?"

"I'll wash it. You go straighten up the bedroom. They didn't touch your things from the way it looks, just pulled the drawers out onto the floor. Don't worry that they had their hands on . . . well . . ."

"My undies? They were just young boys, Spence, playing grown-up games. It's not as though I'm imagining some pervert roaming through my belongings. This is somehow a little easier to take because they were kids. That's dumb, I guess, but I have to find the bright side someplace. Okay, you're floor, I'm bedroom."

"What you are," he said softly, "is wonderful." He stepped into the kitchen and trailed his thumb over her cheek. "Don't change, Tricia. Don't let anyone or anything change you."

"We change all the time, Spence. We never stop changing, growing, not really. There's so much to see, and do, and learn."

"I suppose, but make sure you stay in the sunshine while you're doing all those things."

"In the sunshine?"

"Never mind. Move your cute tush. I've got a floor to wash here. I'm one of the finest floor washers in Denver."

"You're also," she said, "one of the nicest men I've ever met."

He smiled. "That's debatable. Go on. Let's get this finished so you can go to bed. You've had a helluva day."

She gazed up at him for a long moment, then turned and walked slowly from the room. He watched her go as he reached for the mop. After scrubbing the floor to within an inch of its life, he checked the locks on the windows and doors of the kitchen and living room. Then he wandered over to her bedroom and stopped in the doorway. The small room, decorated in white with touches of perky daisies, was in order.

"All set?" he asked.

"Done," she said, "and I'm admittedly exhausted. I don't recommend this as a way to do one's spring cleaning."

He entered the room and checked the lock on the window.

"Keep your windows locked from now on," he said.

"Yes. Yes, I will." How silly, she thought, but she was suddenly nervous. Spence seemed to fill her tiny bedroom to overflowing, his masculinity accentuated by the feminine decor. Her heart was beating like a bongo drum, for Pete's sake. "Well!" she said much too loudly. "I guess that does it."

"Do you have a spare pillow and a blanket or sheet?"

"I knew it," she said, slouching against the dresser. "I just knew it. This is where you tell me you're spending the night on my sofa."

"Bingo," he said.

"Why?"

"Why?" He shook his head. "Her favorite question. Because you've had a gruesome day and it would be very understandable if you had some aftereffects. Nightmares, whatever. I want to be here if you need me, that's all. Pretend you won me in a raffle."

"That's ridiculous. You can't sleep here. I won't be able to sleep if you're sleeping here. I've never had a man sleep here, so you simply can't sleep here."

"Want to run that by me a little slower?"

"Go home, Lieutenant!"

"Sorry, ma'am," he said, grinning, "I'm in one of my 'above and beyond the call of duty' modes. I'm here to protect you from all and everything."

"Ahh, but, Lieutenant," she said, smiling sweetly, "who is going to protect *you* from *me*?"

"Cute," he said. "Very cute. Just bring the blanket and pillow into the living room." He left the bedroom.

"I tried," she said under her breath. "I really don't want that man sleeping here." She'd meant what she'd said. She'd never be able to sleep with a man sleeping . . . Well, she wouldn't go through that spiel again. This was, without a doubt, the most incredible day of her life.

She pulled from the linen closet a sheet, blanket, and pillow, along with a towel and a new disposable razor. Spence took the bundle from her and thanked her politely.

"I'll hurry through my shower," she said, "then you can have the bathroom. I sincerely thank you for helping me clean up this place. Oh, and I hope you sleep well, although you're much too tall for that sofa. If you get hungry, please help yourself to—"

"Tricia," he interrupted.

"Yes?"

"Good night."

"Oh. Yes, well, good night." She spun around and hurried back into the bedroom, closing the door behind her.

Spence chuckled softly and sat down on the sofa. He really wasn't tired, but this was the only way he could get Tricia to end the grueling day she'd had.

The bedroom door opened and a blur of motion sped into the bathroom. He heard the shower a moment later. He leaned back, lacing his fingers behind his head. Soon the water stopped. He waited. In a few minutes Tricia zoomed past.

" 'Night," she called out, then the bedroom door closed behind her once again.

"Good night, sunshine," he said quietly.

After using the bathroom, Spence spread the sheet out on the sofa and took off his shoes and shirt. He placed his gun on the end table, then turned off the light and stretched out on the sofa, staring up into the darkness.

This was a new experience, he thought dryly. Spence Walker sleeping a room away from a desirable woman. Correct that. The *most* desirable woman he'd ever met. But he couldn't leave her, not knowing if she was going to have a delayed reaction to what had happened. It didn't mean he had "heart trouble," as wiseacre Baker put it. He was just a decent person, that was all. No big deal.

So, he'd sleep on the too-short and lumpy sofa and hope that he could still walk in the morning. And hope that the ache of desire in his gut allowed him to get any sleep at all.

With a groan Spence sought a more comfortable position, then gave up the attempt as a lost cause and closed his eyes.

• • •

In the bedroom Tricia lay on her bed with the blankets pulled up to her chin, her eyes wide open.

Spence was out there, she thought wildly. Spence Walker, whose kiss and touch turned her into a blithering idiot, was sleeping in her living room. Naked? He wouldn't dare! He must be a morning shower person, and she was a night shower person, so that worked out well. How nice. Oh, who cared? This was insane. She didn't need a baby-sitter.

Well, she admitted, it was rather comforting to know she wasn't alone right now. But, oh, Lord, the thought of Spence—beautiful, magnificent Spence—being so close, so . . . there, was very hard on the nervous system. Good grief, she sounded like a sex maniac who was about to take a flying leap at Spence's body.

She laughed softly at the image that thought created, then flopped over onto her stomach. The events of the day had finally caught up with her, and with a weary sigh she drifted off to sleep.

Four

A steady thudding noise woke Spence the next morning, and he bolted upright on the sofa. He lost his balance in the process and toppled onto the floor. The air hummed with his colorful expletives. Shaking his head to clear the fogginess of sleep, he glanced quickly around the room.

Sun was streaming in the windows, Tricia's bedroom door was open, and the noise seemed to be coming from the front porch. He strode to the door and flung it open.

"What in the—" he started, then stared in shock at Tricia. "What do you think you're doing?" he bellowed.

"Jumping rope," she said, not looking at him or halting her steady rhythm. "Down in the valley where the green grass grows," she chanted, "lives my lover with the gorgeous toes."

"Tricia!"

"How many toes does my lover have? One, and a two, and a—"

"Tricia!"

"Physical fitness, Spence," she panted. "I'm mushy, remember?"

"Get in this house."

"Don't yell. I lost count of my lover's toes."

"That's enough," he growled, stepping out onto the porch. "You hit me with that thing and I'll take it away from you."

"Police brutality!" she yelled. "One hundred toes." She gasped to a stop. "Done."

"You cheated."

"I did not. You made me lose count. I'm sure I got to a hundred."

"I'd like to meet this guy with the hundred toes. He must have fascinating shoes."

"Oh, he's charming. He's—" Tricia stopped speaking as her gaze swept over Spence's bare chest. She'd totally ignored his inert form as she'd crept past him on her way to the porch, and now here he was in all his bare-chested glory. So tanned, so muscular, with luscious tawny curls that swirled across his chest, then disappeared below the waistband of those tight, tight jeans. Lord above, she couldn't breathe. "Ohh," she said, drawing air into her lungs. "Ohh, I'm dying."

"I think fifty toes would have been plenty for your first attempt," he said. "*Now* will you go in the house? Your bouncing around is a little hard to take first thing in the morning."

She gave him a haughty look and reentered the house. He followed, shaking his head and smiling.

"Well, darn," she said, stopping in the living room, "I messed up the program. I have to shower again. See? It was all organized and I screwed it up. You go ahead and use the bathroom, and I'll make some coffee. Do you eat breakfast?"

"I grab something if I have time. It really doesn't matter. Coffee is fine."

" 'Kay," she said. She watched Spence stride into the bathroom and close the door, then leaned her hand on the end table for support. His back was as marvelous as his chest, she thought dreamily. Sculpted muscles, tanned skin, narrow hips, and the nicest tush she'd ever seen. "Mercy," she said, pressing her hand to her forehead. "Make the coffee, Tricia. Do not think about Spence Walker's muscle tone."

In the shower Spence realized he was humming the ditty about the jerk in the valley with the deformed toes, and snorted in disgust.

Tricia was crazy, he decided. Tricia was adorable. Tricia had also been wearing the skimpy shorts he'd fantasized about, along with a T-shirt that clung to her small breasts. Tricia Todd was driving him out of his mind!

Showered, clean-shaven, and dressed in yesterday's clothes, Spence left the bathroom and headed for the kitchen. The now familiar blur darted out of the bedroom and disappeared into the bathroom. He laughed, then went into the kitchen and poured himself a mug of coffee. The telephone rang. He strode back into the living room and picked up the receiver.

"Walker."

"Walker?" a woman said. "Walker who?"

Uh-oh, Spence thought. Ten bucks said this was Tricia's mother.

"Where's Patricia?" the woman asked.

"She's . . . Um, feeding the cat."

"And who, pray tell, are you?"

"Me? Oh, I'm a friend of hers. I just dropped by to have breakfast with her. We . . . jump rope together. You know, physical fitness, muscle tone. Am I speaking to Tricia's mother?"

"You certainly are, young man. You are young, aren't you? You sound young."

"Compared to what? Or whom? Or whatever."

"Never mind. Your name is Walker?"

"Spence. Spence Walker."

"As in Spencer?"

"Yes."

"Sit tight while I get my book."

"What?" he said. He looked at the receiver, shrugged, and placed it back against his ear.

"Ah-ha," Mrs. Todd said. "Splendid."

"What is?"

"Spencer means 'dispenser of provisions.' Absolutely splendid. That indicates you'll be an excellent provider."

"Oh, now I remember," he said. "Beulah. You're into names. Tricia told me about that."

"Names are extremely important. What do you do for a living?"

"I'm . . . I work for the city."

"Splendid!"

"Thank you. I do my best."

Tricia came out of the bathroom dressed in a

white wraparound skirt and a blue flowered blouse. She glanced at Spence as she fluffed her dark curls.

"Tricia is finished feeding the cat now," he said. "Would you like to speak to her?"

"No, that's all right. Just tell her I'm playing bridge all day and was simply calling to say hello. I wouldn't want to interrupt your . . . exercise. You have a splendid name, Spencer, but you're a lousy liar. Dropped by for breakfast indeed. I'm old, but I'm not stupid. I'm also thrilled to pieces. Go back to what you were doing. 'Bye."

"But . . ." Spence said to the dial tone, then hung up. "Uh-oh."

"Who was that?" Tricia asked, crossing the room.

"Who was who?"

"On the phone."

"Oh, *that* who. Well, that was . . . your mother." He flashed her a dazzling smile.

"What!" Tricia shrieked.

"She's playing bridge today. Ready for some coffee?"

"My mother. My mother? Oh, good Lord, my mother." Her hands flew to her cheeks. "And you told her I was feeding the cat?"

"Well, yeah. I thought it sounded better than my saying you were in the shower. I said I dropped by to jump rope with you and have some breakfast. Oh, and she highly approves of the name Spencer. Want some coffee?"

"Did she believe you?"

"Oh, well, I . . . uh . . ." He shrugged.

"She didn't believe you. She thinks you spent the night. She thinks we're lovers."

"Impossible. I have only ten toes."

"This is not funny, Spencer." She spun around and stomped into the kitchen. Spence was right behind her. "You don't know my wacky mother."

"Hey, I played it close to the cuff, told her I worked for the city instead of saying I was a cop so she wouldn't ask how we met. She didn't seem upset. In fact, she was—"

"Thrilled," Tricia said, rolling her eyes heavenward. "Oh, I know, I know. She's been dreaming of this news flash. I have a lover. The next step is the stroll down the aisle, then she starts knitting booties. She'll inform her bridge club today that her prayers have been answered. Patricia Alida Louise has snagged a man. Oh, I could scream. This is your fault. Quit answering my phone."

"Have some coffee," he said, pouring her a mug full. "Patricia Alida Louise? That's quite a mouthful. Sounds nice, though."

The telephone rang.

"You touch it," Tricia said, glaring at him, "and I'll break your ten toes."

"Beats getting shot in the dingle-dangle," he said, laughing.

"Don't speak to me." She picked up the phone. "Hello? . . . Yes, he is. . . . Certainly. Spence, it's for you."

"Thank you so much," he said, oozing politeness as he took the receiver from her. She stuck her tongue out at him, then went back into the kitchen. "Walker."

"Ted. What's doin'?"

"Nothing."

"Good. Tricia calm down after last night?"

"Yeah, she was great. We cleaned up the place, and I camped out on the sofa."

"Did I ask if you slept with her?"

"No, but I'm telling you I slept on the sofa," Spence said through clenched teeth.

"Right. Okay, listen up, Mr. Paragon-of-Virtue. With all that's happened, I just wanted to make sure you remembered you're to be at Juvenile at ten for Freddy's hearing."

"Yeah, I know," Spence said, sighing. "It ought to be a thrill a minute. I hate being cooped up in those courtrooms."

"You'll live. I'll see you later. Greetings to your lady, Spence."

"She's not my—Hell," he muttered as he realized that Ted had hung up.

Spence walked back into the kitchen and sat down at the table opposite Tricia.

"Have you decided if you're going to take the day off?" he asked. "I think it would do you good to stay here, relax, give yourself a chance to fully recover. What do you think?"

"I think that I . . . um, am not going to my office this morning. This afternoon probably, but definitely not this morning. No, indeed not. Not going there. Nope."

"You're babbling," he said suspiciously.

"Me? I am? Oh. Well, it's because my system is all charged up from jumping rope. Wonderful exercise that rope-jumping. Top notch."

"Tricia, did I miss something here? You're acting very strangely."

"Moi?" She covered her heart with her hand. "I don't feel strange. Do I look strange?"

"No," he said huskily, "you look lovely, absolutely beautiful."

Her "oh" was hardly more than a tiny puff of air.

Their eyes met. They didn't smile, or hardly breathe. They simply looked at each other. Tricia felt a warm flutter in the pit of her stomach. Heat shot through Spence's entire body. He shifted his gaze to his mug.

"I'd better get moving," he said gruffly. "I've got to go home and change clothes."

"Yes, all right," she whispered.

"Ted said to say hello to you." To his lady, he added silently. No, she wasn't his, never would be. Dammit, he knew that, so why did he keep torturing himself with the thought of making love to her? By the time he was ready to settle down, she'd probably be married and have her four kids. Hell, what a depressing thought.

"Ted seems like a nice man," she said.

"What? Oh, yeah, he's great. Good friend, good cop." He stood up. "Listen, don't worry about your mother. We'll come up with something to tell her. I've got to call in and let them know I'm going straight to Juvenile for Freddy's hearing."

Tricia nodded and took a sip of coffee as Spence left the room. Personally, she liked the story her mother believed now, that she and Spence were lovers. But they weren't. When Spence had looked at her a few minutes before, with his blue eyes glowing with such warmth and tenderness, she'd nearly flung herself into his arms. She wanted him to make love to her. She really, really did.

"All set," he said from the kitchen doorway.

She forced herself to smile as she got to her feet. "I'll walk you to the door."

"Are you okay?"

"Yes, of course."

He drew her into his arms, frowning down at her. "You look sad or something," he said.

"No, I'm really all right. It's just that a lot has happened very quickly. I don't mean just Freddy and my house being broken into. It's you, too, Spence, and the way you make me feel. Some of it is very confusing. And most of it is wonderful. Are you planning on kissing me today?"

He groaned. "Your honesty is going to put me in an early grave."

"I don't know how to be any other way."

"I realize that. Yes, I'm going to kiss you today. Then my mind is going to make sweet, sweet love to you, but my body isn't."

"I see," she said, sighing.

"I doubt that you do. Tricia, I want to make love to you so badly I hurt, but I just can't. I know you said you weren't necessarily . . . well, saving yourself for the man you'll marry, but I'm so afraid that deep within you, you really are. I couldn't handle it if you regretted what we shared. I have to do what I feel is the right thing. Understand?"

"No," she said. She decided immediately that she sounded like a pouting four-year-old, but she didn't care.

"Damn. Tricia, listen, we met at the wrong time, that's all. I'm just not at the time in my life when I want to marry and settle down."

"So, who asked you to?" she muttered. Definitely four years old. "I have some rights here, too, you know. I'm an intelligent woman, not overly organized, but intelligent. I make my own decisions. And furthermore, my socially unacceptable virginity is none of your business."

"The hell it isn't, lady," he said, gripping her upper arms.

"Don't yell. My head hurts. Jumping rope gave me a headache. I'm beginning to think I'll never find the right exercise for my muscle tone."

He chuckled and shook his head. "This is where I came in. You shouldn't tempt me with openers like that."

"What?"

"Never mind. Enough of this, okay? I'm going to kiss you now."

"I'm glad."

"Good."

The kiss was powerful, sensuous, and long. Tricia was trembling when Spence finally released her, and his heart was hammering in his chest. He slowly relinquished his hold on her and stepped back.

"How about dinner tonight?" he asked. His voice was hoarse. "I can pick you up at your office at five."

Unable to speak, she nodded, then walked him to the door. He smiled slightly as he trailed his thumb over her cheek, then left the cottage. She watched as he drove away.

"I need a butterscotch ball," she said aloud. "I need six butterscotch balls."

In the kitchen she flung open a cupboard and pulled out a bag of candy. After chomping a half dozen of the treats, she decided she felt much better and went to the telephone to make a call.

"Kathy!" she said brightly when her sister answered the phone. "How's my favorite sister?"

"I'm your only sister, Patricia Alida Louise, and that is your you-want-something voice."

"Honestly! A person can't even be a thoughtful sister around here. You'd better be nice to me, Kathy, or I'll tell Mom that I think Beulah is a terrific name for the baby."

"You'd do that to me? A defenseless, fat, pregnant woman? You're cold, Tricia."

"I'm desperate. I need to borrow that trench coat of Chuck's without you asking me why I want it."

"Chuck's trench coat? I stuck it in the back of the closet, because every time he wears it he feels compelled to do an impersonation of Humphrey Bogart. A lousy impersonation. He has that god-awful fedora too."

"Perfect," Tricia said.

"No, absurd. Why do you want—"

"You can't ask, remember? I'll be over in a jiffy to get them."

"Patricia Todd, what are you up to? Why aren't you going to work? Are you in some kind of trouble?"

"Kathy, you'll upset Beulah if you don't calm down. See you in a bit. 'Bye." She hung up before Kathy could get another word in.

• • •

Spence shifted his weight and leaned back against the wall, folding his arms loosely over his chest. It was hot in the courtroom and the tie he was wearing was strangling him. The room was packed with junior hoods and their parents, and things were running behind schedule. Damn that Freddy.

The door opened and Spence glanced over there, dreading the thought of more people squeezing into the already crowded courtroom. He did a double-take as a strange figure entered the room. The man sat down on a bench in the back, receiving annoyed glares from the people who had to move over to make room for him.

Weird, Spence thought. The guy was decked out in a trench coat about three sizes too big, a floppy fedora pulled low over his face, and huge sunglasses. Or at least he assumed it was a guy. There was really no telling in that get-up. There were some strange people in this town.

"Case number three two nine," the clerk called. "Frederick Jackson."

Finally, Spence thought. He pushed himself away from the wall and walked to the front of the courtroom.

Thank heavens she wasn't too late, Tricia thought. Kathy hadn't been able to remember where she'd put Chuck's fedora, and had used the time she'd spent searching for it to quiz Tricia unmercifully as to what she was up to. Tricia had refused to say a word.

"Lieutenant Walker," the clerk asked, "do you have the police report on Frederick Jackson?"

"Yes," Spence said. He handed the man the papers, and he passed them on to the judge.

Tricia sat up straighter. Goodness, she thought, Spence Walker in a sport coat and slacks was something to behold, even from the back. Those shoulders! Those narrow hips, those long, long muscular legs— Enough. She had to pay attention. Freddy didn't look too terrific. He really did need a haircut, and his jeans and T-shirt were overdue for a washing. He was so small compared to Spence. Well, Freddy was just a boy and Spence was a man. Yes, indeedy, Spence was definitely a man.

Oh, stop, Tricia told herself. She wasn't there to gawk at Spence. Lord, she was roasting. She'd bet that Humphrey Bogart hadn't melted into a grease spot when he'd worn his trench coat. This was the pits.

"Mrs. Jackson?" the judge said to the woman standing next to Freddy. She was short and plump, and had streaks of gray in her dark hair. "Is Mr. Jackson with you?"

"No, sir," she said in a trembling voice. "He left us years ago. I have five children and Freddy is the oldest, the man of the house. He's a good boy, your honor. He worked after school to help put food on the table. He graduated from high school and—"

"Thank you, Mrs. Jackson," the judge interrupted, smiling at her. "Now then, Frederick," he went on, his expression stern, "it appears you've gotten yourself into trouble."

No joke, Spence thought dryly.

Well, Tricia thought, just an itsy-bitsy, teeny-tiny bit.

"Yeah," Freddy said sullenly.

"Pardon me?" the judge said.

"Yes, sir."

"Lieutenant Walker feels that you're involved with a street gang, and the incidents you've taken part in are connected with your initiation. Would you care to comment on that?"

"No, sir."

Figures, Spence thought.

Freddy is loyal to his friends, Tricia thought. Crumb-bums that they were.

"This report," the judge continued, "states that you pointed a gun, granted an unloaded gun, at an innocent woman on the stairway of a building and threatened to shoot her."

"Innocent woman!" Freddy said. "That was a cop, Walker's partner. She had a gun, too, and she said she'd shoot me in the dingle-dangle."

"Oh!" Tricia gasped.

Spence stiffened. The hair on the back of his neck stood up and every muscle in his body tensed. Tricia! he thought. He would swear that that astonished-sounding "oh" had been her voice. No, that was nuts. She was tucked away in her little cottage. Wasn't she? Oh, Lord, if she was in this room he'd wring her neck. She'd said she was staying home all morning. Wait a minute. What she'd actually said was that she wasn't going to the office!

He turned his head slightly to try to get a look

at the people behind him. Tricia slouched lower on the bench.

"No, Frederick," the judge said, drawing Spence's attention back to the front of the room, "that woman was not a police officer, and the gun in her hand was a toy. You frightened her, threatened her, caused her a great deal of distress."

Damn right, Spence fumed.

Not a great deal, Tricia thought. Just a tad.

"Yes, sir," Freddy said. "Sorry, sir."

"It's very easy," the judge went on, "for you to stand here and apologize for your actions. That isn't good enough. I'm assigning you to a counselor of the court, whom you will meet with once a week for the next three months. You're on probation for those three months, during which time you are to have no association with the members of the street gang you're connected with. Should you be seen in their presence, you will be in violation of probation and will reappear before me for sentencing. Any questions?"

"No, sir," Freddy said, then clicked his tongue in disgust.

The judge cocked an eyebrow. "Young man, you're getting off very lightly here. Don't push your luck. Stop in the main office on the way out for the information regarding your counseling sessions. Next case."

Freddy spun around and his face was dark with anger as he stomped down the aisle. His mother followed, sniffling into a hankie. Spence was next, already tugging at the knot of his tie. Tricia peered over her shoulder at the group as they left the courtroom, and when they were safely out of the room, she slid off the bench. Poking her head out the door, she looked up and down the hall.

Okay, she thought, there were Freddy and his mother going into that office. Check. But where was Spence? The last thing she needed was to run smack-dab into him. Her disguise was good, but she'd prefer not to put it to the maximum test.

Taking a deep breath, she stepped out into the hall. No Spence. Adopting what she hoped was a masculine stride, she tucked her chin farther into her upturned collar and walked in the direction Freddy and his mother had gone. Close to the office door, she stopped at a drinking fountain and bent over it, sipping the cool water.

Spence replaced the receiver on the pay phone and strode around the corner in time to see the trench coat—clad man going down the hall. Weird, he thought again. The guy looked like Dopey the Dwarf. He also looked vaguely familiar. There was just . . . something about him that struck a chord. Forget it. He had better things to do with his mental energies.

He went back into the courtroom and scanned the crowd. No Tricia. But neither had there been a Tricia at home or at her office. Damn, he could have sworn that gasp he'd heard had come from her. Well, guess not. But where was she?

Back in the hall, he glanced again at the trench-coat—clad man, who was now getting a drink of water, then turned in the opposite direction and left the building.

•   •   •

She was drowning, Tricia thought. If she drank
any more water, she was going to explode. Freddy
and his mother were now right behind her in the
hall, and Mrs. Jackson was still crying, saying
Freddy had always been such a good boy.

"Ma, please," Freddy said, "that's enough, okay?
I didn't get sentenced to San Quentin, you know."

"You've got to stay away from those hoodlums,
Freddy."

"Yeah, yeah, I know. Look, you go on to work
before you lose any more time. I'll talk to you at
home tonight."

"What are you going to do?"

"I'll buy a paper and see what jobs are listed. I
can't help it that they cut back at the grocery
store, but I'll find something else. No more tears,
Ma. Everything is going to be all right. I love you,
Ma."

Oh, how sweet, Tricia thought, then choked on
a gulp of water.

"I love you, too, Freddy," Mrs. Jackson said.
"I've got to hurry. I'll see you tonight."

"Yeah," Freddy said.

Tricia moved her head to watch Mrs. Jackson
leave, only to have the water drench her sunglasses.

"Darn," she said, straightening and taking them
off. She turned to face Freddy. "Pssst."

"Shove off," Freddy said. "Panhandle someplace
else. I don't have a dime."

"Freddy, it's me."

"Me who?" he asked, eyeing her warily.

She yanked off the hat. "Me, Tricia Todd. You
know, from the stairs in the building? You thought

I was Lieutenant Walker's partner, but I'm not. I'm the one who threatened to shoot you in the . . . place I said. Do you remember me now?"

"Who could forget?" he muttered. "You scared the hell out of me with that gun. I thought you were a cop."

"I'm a CPA."

"You look like a bag lady. What do you want? I've had enough hassles in this place."

"I want to help you," she said, smiling brightly.

He narrowed his eyes. "Help me do what?"

"Whatever you want to do."

"So, who are you? The tooth fairy? Hell, I'm standing here talking to a nut case dressed like Sam Spade. I've had enough of this." He started to move past her.

"Freddy, wait, please," Tricia said, placing her hand on his arm. "I'm wearing this disguise so Lieutenant Walker won't recognize me."

"Oh?" Freddy said, stopping. "You're hiding out from Walker?"

"Well, sort of."

"You're a crooked CPA and he's trying to nail you, right?"

"No! Spence and I— That is, Lieutenant Walker and I are . . . friends. If he knew I'd come down here to talk to you, he'd pitch a fit."

"Oh, I get it. You're Walker's lady. I still don't know what you want."

"I'm not exactly his . . . Never mind. Freddy, I haven't been able to get you out of my mind since what happened on the stairs. After hearing what was said in that courtroom, I'm even more convinced that you're a decent young man. It's obvious that you've been shouldering some tremendous responsibilities at home."

"So? What's it to you?"

"I want to be your friend. I want to help you find a job, get yourself back on track."

"'Sure, you do," he said with a snort of disgust. "At what price?"

"I don't want anything from you, Freddy. I lost my father when I was fifteen, but I never lacked for anything. I guess I'm trying to give back some of what I was so lucky to have. I can't believe you really want to see your mother cry anymore."

A flicker of pain crossed Freddy's face, but he quickly controlled his emotions and gave Tricia a hard stare.

"You're out to reform me, huh?" he said, a cold edge to his voice. "But Walker wouldn't like it, not one damn bit. He thinks I'm scum. All the cops think anyone from my part of town is scum. Hell, what a scam! Pulling a fast one on Walker with his lady, right under his nose. And all straight-up legal. Man, I love it. It's time somebody took that hotshot cop down a peg or two."

"Your attitude leaves a lot to be desired," Tricia muttered.

"I'm all yours," Freddy said, grinning and spreading his arms wide.

She planted her hands on her hips. "Fine. As of right now, you and I are partners. Just remember, you can't pick and choose which of my directives you wish to follow. It's all or nothing. Deal?" She extended her hand.

"To get back at Walker? Lady, you can be a

do-gooder from here to Sunday," he said, shaking her hand.

"I've got to work on his attitude," she said under her breath.

"So, when do we start reforming me?"

"Right now, Mr. Jackson. You're about to get a haircut."

"Ah, hell!"

Five

By late afternoon Tricia, back in her office, was a wreck. She'd eaten so many butterscotch balls in an attempt to calm her jangled nerves, her jaw ached. She was excited over her accomplishments of the morning—meeting Freddy, convincing him to cooperate with her, then the subsequent haircut.

And she had a knot the size of a bowling ball in the pit of her stomach, fearful that Spence would discover what she'd done.

The argument in her mind began yet again, the back and forth dialogue between herself and herself that was driving her, as Spence would say, ba-nan-as.

She was an adult, she told herself, and she could do as she pleased regarding Freddy.

But, herself answered back, Spence would be furious that she'd sought out, then established a partnership of sorts with the junior hood, whom Spence had no fondness for whatsoever. An angry

Spence Walker was a Spence Walker Tricia had no desire to cross swords with.

So? Let Spence stew. She wasn't accountable to him for her actions.

But she wanted to be! She wanted to be an important part of his life and vice versa. And, yes, she wanted to make love with him. If he found out about Freddy, he was liable to make war, not love.

"Oh," she moaned, and popped another butterscotch ball into her mouth. Freddy was important to her. There was just something about him that had touched her deeply. For all his cocky, belligerent exterior, she knew, she just knew, he was a sensitive, frightened, decent young man.

She smiled as she recalled the look of horror on his face when she'd ushered him into the beauty salon she patronized rather than a barber shop. He'd nearly bolted for the door when the beautician had started to drape a pink plastic cape around him, but Tricia had patted his hand and said to trust her. His curse had brought gasps and looks of disdain from the other patrons in the shop, but Tricia had smiled at them and told the beautician to proceed.

"I'll be damned," Freddy had said when the haircut was completed. He'd leaned closer to the mirror and turned his head from side to side.

"It's fantastic," Tricia had said, beaming. "Your hair is gorgeous, Freddy. It's so dark and shiny and thick. Perfect."

"I'd give a million to have your eyelashes, Freddy," the beautician had said.

"Yeah?" He'd grinned. "My eyelashes?"

"You bet," the woman had said. "If I were thirty years younger, I'd be chasing you down the block, you heartbreaker you."

Tricia had felt a warm glow curl within her when a flush of embarrassment stained Freddy's cheeks. "Thank you, ma'am," he'd mumbled.

Oh, yes, Tricia thought, sinking back in her chair, Freddy Jackson was special, and worth every effort she made to get him on the right road. Given time, she was sure she could convince Spence of that too. But just how much time did she have with Spence? What was he thinking? What were his plans regarding his involvement with her? She didn't know.

She opened the file on her desk, glanced at the papers, then stared into space again. Where was Spence? she wondered. What was he doing?

And where was Freddy? Was he having any luck in his search for a job? Over lunch at a small café, they had circled the possibilities in the ads. One thing was certain—there was nothing wrong with Freddy Jackson's appetite. He'd devoured three hamburgers and two huge slices of chocolate cake before deciding he'd had enough.

Freddy had no real skills, Tricia mused, and was capable of only manual labor that paid minimum wage. True, any job was better than none, but maybe he had a dream, some secret wish for his future. She'd talk to him about that once she got closer to him. And once she'd straightened out his attitude! His reformation was a game to him, a way to put one over on Spence. Well, she'd just see about that!

Spence, her mind and heart echoed. He was

America's most popular, most compelling romance novels...

Here, at last...love stories that really involve you!
Fresh, finely crafted novels with story lines so
believable you'll feel you're actually living them!
Characters you can relate to...exciting places to
visit...unexpected plot twists...all in all, exciting
romances that satisfy your mind and delight
your heart.

EXAMINE 4
LOVESWEPT NOVELS FOR
15 Days FREE!

To introduce you to this fabulous service, you'll get four brand-
new Loveswept releases not yet in the bookstores. These four
exciting new titles are yours to examine for 15 days without
obligation to buy. Keep them if you wish for just $9.95 plus
postage and handling and any applicable sales tax.

☐ **YES,** please send me four new romances for a 15-day
FREE examination. If I keep them, I will pay just $9.95 plus
postage and handling and any applicable sales tax and you will
enter my name on your preferred customer list to receive all four
new Loveswept novels published each month *before* they are
released to the bookstores—always on the same 15-day free
examination basis.

20123

Name_____

Address_____

City_____

State_____ Zip_____

My Guarantee: I am never required to buy any shipment unless I
wish. I may preview each shipment for 15 days. If I don't want it, I
simply return the shipment within 15 days and owe nothing for it.

R 2234

Now you can be sure you'll never, ever miss a single Loveswept title by enrolling in our special reader's home delivery service. A service that will bring all four new Loveswept romances published every month into your home—and deliver them to you before they appear in the bookstores!

Examine 4 Loveswept Novels for

15 days FREE!

(SEE OTHER SIDE FOR DETAILS)

always in her thoughts, causing a delicious warmth within her. If only he weren't so stubborn, so determined to protect her from him. If only he would move the timetable up on his emotions, and be ready for love and commitment *now*. If only he would fall in love with her, just as she had fallen in love with him.

Tricia sat bolt upright, her heart pounding wildly. She loved Spence? she asked herself. *Loved* him?

"I love him," she said, deciding to try it out loud to see how it sounded. She smiled. "I do. Oh, yes, I'm in love with Spence. I'm so disorganized, I didn't even realize that I'd fallen in love."

She stood and walked over to the windows, her arms wrapped around herself. Dark clouds were beginning to build on the horizon, and she wondered absently if it was going to rain. Traffic surged along Broadway in the usual late afternoon rush to get home, and eerie shadows flickered over the tall buildings. It was a familiar scene, one Tricia had gazed at countless times. But now it seemed different, changed, because *she* was no longer whom she had been.

She was a woman in love.

"Well," she said. "Fancy that." There were so many emotions churning within her, it was a wonder there was room for them all. There was awe, and joy, and excitement, and desire. And there was a coiling knot of dread that this love would leave her with a shattered heart.

She lifted her chin as she watched the storm clouds roll across the darkening sky. Before Spence left her, before she cried, she would have her memories to keep. She would be one with Spence Walker. She would convince Spence that she controlled her own destiny, made her own choices. He wouldn't feel any obligation toward her, or any guilt. She would go to him willingly, lovingly, and when he left, she'd bid him a quiet farewell.

With a decisive nod she returned to her desk and her work. She was Patricia Todd, CPA. She was Tricia, woman in love.

Thunder rumbled through the heavens, and just before five o'clock the storm hit in a torrent of rain that made it nearly impossible to see out the windows. Was Spence dry and warm? Tricia wondered. Was Freddy? Surely they had enough sense to stay out of the rain. Didn't they?

Ten minutes later one of her questions was answered. The door was flung open and Spence entered her office. He was wet, thoroughly soaked, and dripping water on the carpet.

"Good grief," she said. "You look like a drowned rat." Oh, he was beautiful! And she loved him. Yes, yes, yes, she loved this man. "Aren't you cold?"

"You could say that," he said in disgust. "Tell me you have an umbrella in that bottomless bag of yours, or I'll have to go buy you one before you try to get to the car. I got this soaked just running to the building. Do you have an umbrella?"

"Yes."

"Good. Do you mind if I use your phone? Lord, I'm wet."

As Spence made his call, Tricia unplugged the coffeepot and straightened her desk so she'd be ready to leave when he got off the phone. She ignored what he was saying to whomever he was talking to, but couldn't resist stealing glances at him out of the corner of her eye. His sodden clothes stuck to him like a second skin, outlining to perfection his muscled physique. Her heart skipped a beat or two as she gazed at him, and a feathery sensation whispered along her spine. He raked a hand through his wet hair, and she imagined her fingers following the same path.

"Mercy," she said under her breath as desire swept through her.

"Yeah, okay," Spence said into the phone. "I'll check in later." He replaced the receiver and turned to Tricia. "Where were you?"

Uh-oh, she thought. "Where was I when?" she asked, all innocence.

"This morning," he said, frowning. "I called the cottage and here, but you weren't at either place."

"Oh, *that* when. Well, I—I had an errand to run. You must have just missed me."

"I thought you were going to take it easy, relax."

"Some errands can't be postponed, Spence."

"Yeah, I suppose. I'm surprised you haven't asked what happened to Freddy at his hearing."

"What happened to Freddy at the hearing?" she asked in a rush. Darn it, she fumed, if she was going to be a sneaking-in-the-shadows type she'd have to get organized.

"A slap on the wrist," he said. "He goes to counseling for three months and stays away from the street gang. He got off light."

What he got, Tricia thought smugly, was a haircut, a huge meal, and a list of jobs to apply for. "I'm sure the judge knew what he was doing."

Spence shrugged. "Who knows? Time will tell. Are you ready to go?"

"Yes." She rummaged through her bag. "Keys. Umbrella. Want a butterscotch ball?"

He chuckled. "No thanks. I'll settle for dry clothes and a hot meal. Why don't we go to my place so I can change, then decide what we want to do about dinner? We'll leave your car here for now. Okay?"

His place? she thought wildly. "Fine," she said, hoping she was smiling. Spence's place? Where he lived? And slept? In a bed? Of course, in a bed, stupid. Everyone had a bed . . . for sleeping. Oh, Lord.

"Tricia?"

"What?"

"You have a strange look on your face."

"That's hunger. I'm hungry. For food," she added quickly. "Really starved."

"Right," he said skeptically.

"I'm sure you're hungry . . . for food. Oh, for Pete's sake." She walked to the door. "Let's go."

"What is your problem?" he asked, following behind her.

"Nothing," she yelled, yanking open the door. "Oh," she gasped as she nearly collided with the attractive young woman on the other side. "Hi, Shawna."

"Hi," Shawna said. "I have to work overtime and I ran out of sugar for my coffee. Do you have some I can borrow? Oh, hello," she added, looking past Tricia at Spence.

"Hello," he said, smiling.

"Shawna O'Neal, this is Spence Walker," Tricia said. "I'll get you some sugar."

"I'll help you," Shawna said, following close on Tricia's heels. When they reached the coffeepot in the corner of the office, Shawna leaned close to Tricia. "Who is he?" she whispered. "He's one gorgeous hunk of stuff. Tell me he isn't just a client of yours."

"He isn't a client. Here's your sugar."

"Then who is he? Oh, he's beautiful, even sopping wet. No wonder you were never interested in the guys I wanted to fix you up with. You've been holding out on me, Tricia. Not that I blame you. I wouldn't trust me around your Spence either. Good Lord, what a body on him."

"Shawna, for heaven's sake!"

"I'll leave so you can proceed with whatever you were going to proceed with," Shawna said. "And I will definitely talk to you tomorrow, Tricia Todd."

"You do that," Tricia said as they walked to the door. " 'Bye, Shawna."

" 'Bye. Nice meeting you, Spence."

"I certainly made *her* day," Tricia muttered as Shawna returned to her office down the hall.

"Let's go," Spence said. "I'm frozen to the bone."

"Oh, I'm sorry. After you, Lieutenant."

Out in the corridor, she locked the door, he checked it, then they started toward the elevator.

"Have a wonderful evening," Shawna called from the end of the hall. "Don't you just adore rainy nights? They're so cozy."

"Good-bye, Shawna," Tricia called back. "Her mother should have named her 'Jobina,' " she said to Spence. "It means 'the afflicted.' Shawna is so cuckoo, she's exhausting."

Tricia's umbrella was nearly useless against the

pounding rain, and she was wet and cold by the time she and Spence got into his car. He turned on the heater, and they drove in silence, Spence concentrating on trying to see through the downpour. Twenty minutes later he pulled into the underground garage of a high-rise apartment building. In the elevator he tucked Tricia close to his side.

"You're chilly," he said. "You need to get out of those wet things."

She opened her mouth to reply, then snapped it shut again. Take her clothes off? she asked silently. In Spence's apartment? She couldn't do that. Yes, she could. Of course she could, because she had every intention of making love with him. If she didn't have a heart attack first.

Spence's apartment was a good size and had a welcoming feel to it. The sofa and chairs were large, appropriate for a man of his build, and the color scheme was brown with accents of blue.

"This is a lovely apartment," she said.

"Thanks. We'd better get organized. You shower first. I have a robe my aunt sent me one Christmas you can put on. I'll see what's in the kitchen to eat."

"Oh, well, I'm not that wet. Why don't you shower first?"

"Nope." He strode into the bedroom and returned a minute later with a blue velour bathrobe. "Here you go. The bathroom is at the end of the hall."

She took the robe, managed a small smile, and hurried toward the bathroom. She snuck a peek into Spence's bedroom as she passed it, and her heart raced at the sight of his king-size bed.

How many women . . . she began to wonder. No, it didn't matter. *She* was here now. She was here and she loved him. That was all that mattered. So far she was acting like a ridiculous child, but she was getting her act together. Right now.

To Tricia's dismay she discovered that even her bra and panties were damp from the rain, and with phony bravado she draped the lacy lingerie over the towel rod. She spread her skirt, blouse, and slip on the hamper and sink, then stepped into the shower. She was warm and tingling when she dried with a fluffy towel and pulled on the robe.

"Good grief," she said. "It's huge." The sleeves hung far below her hands and she had to hike up what seemed like yards of material even to walk. "Femme fatale you're not, kid. Oh, well." She went in search of Spence and found him peering into a kitchen cupboard. "I'm finished with the shower, Spence."

"Okay. How does tomato soup and grilled cheese sandwiches sound?" he asked, taking a can of soup from the cupboard.

"Fine."

"I'll shower, then—" He stopped speaking as he turned to face her. Lord, she was beautiful, he thought. So fresh and enchanting. His shower had better be ice cold, and he should get to it fast.

She laughed. "I know. I look silly. This robe is enormous."

"You look"—he cleared his throat—"fine. Oversized clothes are very in this year. There was a guy at Juvenile this morning wearing a trench coat that fit him about like that."

She smiled weakly. "You don't say. Maybe he has a thing for Humphrey Bogart."

"Or something." Spence inched around her without touching her and strode quickly from the room.

She frowned at his hasty departure, then decided he was just eager to get out of his wet things. She attempted to roll up the sleeves on the robe, but the thick, soft fabric refused to cooperate.

Rubber bands, she thought. She had some in her bag, she was sure of it. So, where was her bag? Oh, yes, she'd left it in the hall outside the bathroom door.

She hiked up the robe, and padded across the living room and down the hall. Just as she bent down to pick up her bag, the bathroom door opened. The scent of soap drifted into the hall as the steamy air escaped from the bathroom. Spence was standing motionless in the doorway, wearing only a towel tucked low on his hips.

She was staring directly at his muscle-corded legs, which were covered by moist tawny hair. As she slowly straightened, her body seemed heavy, requiring all her energy to get upright. And as she moved, she missed no detail of the magnificent body in front of her.

Spence was riveted in place. His skin seemed to burn as Tricia's gaze swept over him; up and up, to at last meet his eyes when she stood erect. His heart thundered in his chest, the blood pounded in his veins, but still he didn't move.

The memory of her wispy bra and panties hanging on the towel rod slammed into his brain, causing a stirring in the lower regions of his body as he realized she was naked beneath his robe. He imagined slipping the robe from her silken body and gathering her into his arms, and his hands curled into tight fists as he continued to gaze into the dark pools of her eyes.

A wondrous yearning grew within Tricia. Heat flared in a deep, secret place within her, then spread throughout all of her body. Her breasts felt heavy as her nipples hardened, and she ached for Spence's soothing touch.

Desire, excitement, and fear tumbled in confusion inside her. But with them also came the knowledge that she loved this man. It was time, time to give herself to him in love. A calmness crept in around the churning passion within her, and she smiled.

"Spence," she said. Her voice was husky with desire. It was only one word, but combined with her gentle smile and the love shining in her eyes, it spoke volumes.

Spence sucked in his breath as though he'd just been punched. His muscles ached from his rigid stance as he fought the battle raging in his mind.

"No," he said harshly. "You don't understand. I'm the wrong man, Tricia."

"I do understand," she whispered. "More than you realize. I want you, Spence. I'm not asking for promises, or commitments, or tomorrows. I've made my decision. Now you have to make yours. Do you want me? Do you, Spence?"

The little voice in his mind screamed for his attention, telling him that Tricia was not his to have. She was innocence and sunshine, and deserved better than what he could offer her.

"Don't you want me, Spence?"

Tricia's voice flowed over and through him, warming him, then heating his desire to a fever pitch. He beat that inner voice into submission and silence.

"I want you, Tricia,' he said. "You don't know how much I want you."

"Then come to me, Spence."

With a strangled moan he lifted her into his arms. His mouth captured hers and she clung to him, feverishly returning his kiss. He lifted his head and gazed at her for a long moment, then carried her into the bedroom.

He set her on her feet, swept back the blankets on the bed, then gently drew her back into his embrace.

"Let me just hold you for a minute," he said, his voice vibrant with emotion. "I don't want to rush you. This has got to be perfect for you. Perfect! But I need a minute."

She leaned against him, feeling his muscles tremble as he strove for control. She inhaled his soapy, fresh aroma as she gazed at the curly hair on his chest. Without thinking she leaned forward and flicked her tongue over his bare skin. He stiffened, his hands pressing harder on her back. She slowly slid her own hands up his chest, cocking her head to one side in fascination as she explored the contours of his rock-hard body.

"So beautiful," she murmured.

His hands shaking, he pulled the sash free from

the robe and brushed the material from her shoulders. The robe fell in a soft heap onto the floor.

"Oh, Lord," he said hoarsely, his gaze sweeping over her. "You're exquisite." He cupped her breasts in his hands, his thumbs trailing across the nipples and bringing them to an almost painful hardness. "Lovely."

She gasped as he bent his head and drew one taut nipple into his mouth. He suckled rhythmically, and sensations rocketed through her, pulsing with the same cadence as Spence's mouth on her soft flesh. She dropped her head back and closed her eyes to savor the pleasure surging through her. He moved to her other breast, and she clung to his arms for support, a sigh escaping from her lips.

Spence reluctantly withdrew from her as he felt his control slipping. He lifted her onto the cool sheets, drinking in the sight of her as he towered above her. Their eyes met, and he dropped the towel to the floor.

Slowly, slowly she drew her gaze down over him, and her breathing quickened.

He stood motionless, watching, waiting for any flicker of fear or indecision to cross her face. Instead, he saw the wonder in her expression, heard her tiny gasp of excitement. A shudder ripped through him as she smiled at him.

He groaned. "Tricia," he murmured, then laid down next to her, and claimed her mouth in a searing kiss.

When he lifted his head, a deep frown knitted his brows together as he searched her face for reassurance.

"You've got to be certain this is what you want," he said. "The voice in my head is telling me this is wrong, but I want you so damn much. Stop me now, Tricia, or it's going to be too late."

"Love me, Spence," she said. "It's right, and good, and I promise you I won't be sorry. Please, Spence, love me."

He murmured her name, then closed his mouth over one of her breasts, paying homage to her beauty. His hand trailed down her body, lingering on her flat stomach, then moved to the treasured place between her thighs. Where his hand journeyed, his lips followed, his breathing rough as he fought to hold himself in check.

Tricia moved instinctively under his tantalizing foray, arching her back, lifting her hips to seek more of his touch. She was awash with desire, burning with an unknown need. A sob escaped from her.

"Oh, Spence."

"Soon. This is for you, Tricia. I want this to be perfect for you."

Her hands roamed restlessly over his moist skin, and he trembled beneath her touch. She ached with a sweet pain, was suspended between the need to laugh and cry.

"Please," she gasped.

He quickly prepared himself, then moved over her, resting on his forearms as he gazed down at her passion-flushed face.

"I'll try not to hurt you," he said hoarsely. "Hold on to me, Tricia. Just hold on."

"Yes."

He pressed against her, feeling her resistance to

the hard intrusion of his manhood. He entered her slowly, clenching his teeth in his effort to restrain himself, to give her body time to adjust. She was so small, and he was certain he was going to hurt her.

Tricia felt him tense, knew he was hesitating, and panic swept through her. He mustn't stop now! she thought. He mustn't leave her. She wanted this, wanted him. Oh, Spence.

She wrapped her arms around him and thrust her hips upward with all the strength she possessed.

"No!" he said loudly.

A white-hot pain shot through her and she swallowed the cry before it could escape from her lips. As soon as it had come, the pain subsided.

"Yes," she said on a sigh. "Oh, yes."

Spence moved fully into her, sheathing himself in her velvety warmth, feeling as though his soul were passing from him into her.

They were one. Their bodies—one hard and strong, the other soft and supple—surged and danced together, faster and faster as they soared ever higher.

Tricia clung to Spence as she became enveloped in a hazy mist of sensuality. Her heartbeat thundered as she sensed she was nearing some magical summit. She struggled for more, calling to Spence to take her where she wanted, needed to go. And then she was there.

"Spence!"

"Yes, yes, that's it. Don't be afraid. I'm here, Tricia. Go with everything you're feeling. Take it all."

"Oh, Spence."

Rapturous sensations swept through her in rippling waves as her body tightened around him, sending him over the brink. He cried out, joining her in ecstasy, then collapsing on top of her. He lay still for a minute, then pushed himself up to look down at her.

"Tricia?"

She slowly opened her eyes. "Hmm?"

"Don't do that to me. Say something. I know I hurt you, but . . ."

"No. Oh, Spence, it was so . . . I feel so . . . you are so . . ."

"Tricia!"

"Wonderful." She smiled. "I never dreamed it would be so wonderful."

"Oh, thank God," he said, and buried his face in the fragrant cloud of her hair. "Are you sure?" he asked when he lifted his head again. "Damn, I sound like an insecure kid. But I wanted it to be so special for you. I didn't mean to hurt you like that, but you sort of took matters into your own hands. I'd better get off you."

"Oh, don't go. You feel so good inside me."

"At the moment maybe. Your body might complain later about this momentous step you took, though."

"I'm not sorry, Spence. I'll never be sorry. I promised you that, and I meant it."

He kissed her then and she tangled her fingers in his thick hair. He'd never get enough of her, he thought, feeling the renewed stirrings of his manhood as their tongues entwined. Never. As he filled her body, she filled his soul. She was rare. She was sunshine. She was his.

And he loved her.

No, you fool, his little voice screamed. He didn't have room in his life for love. Not now, not yet. This wasn't the time, he wasn't ready. He couldn't be in love with her.

Yes, his heart whispered. He loved Tricia Todd.

"Tricia," he said, finally ending the passionate kiss, "no more."

"You want me. I can feel you, feel how much you want me."

"It's too much too soon. You have to take this slower."

"Why?"

"Why! I'm going to have that word declared illegal. Because I'm a big man, and you're a small woman and . . . because you're going to be sore as hell. How's that for blunt?"

"Oh," she said, running her tongue over his bottom lip. Her hands roamed across his back, then lower. She danced her fingertips across his taut buttocks.

"Tricia, are you listening to me?"

"No." She slid her hand between them and felt his stomach muscles jump. "Such marvelous muscle tone you have. What kind of exercise did you say you preferred?"

"I'm not going to make love to you again tonight, understand? I'm moving off you right now. Got that? Dammit, Tricia, get your hand out of there! You're driving me crazy."

"Hmm?" she said, smiling.

"Oh, hell, forget it."

Again they soared, and again they toppled over the edge of reality, calling to each other. Afterward, Spence moved away and cradled Tricia close to his side, pulling the sheet over their cooling bodies. She sighed in contentment, then drifted off to sleep. He wove his fingers through her curls and stared at her delicate face.

He loved her, he thought. How in hell had *that* happened? *He* controlled his life, his future, his emotions. How could a tiny whisper of a woman push his buttons like this? He didn't like it, not one damn bit.

Well, just because he'd fallen in love didn't mean he had to do anything about it, he decided. A man had to follow through on love to have it mean something. He had to make a commitment, declare his feelings for the woman. He'd do neither, and that would be that. The love he felt for Tricia would dissolve . . . eventually. But for now he was in love—and it was scary as hell.

He felt stripped bare and vulnerable as he realized that until he regained control of his emotions, Tricia had the power to crumble him into dust. No, he didn't like this at all. Maybe he would never be ready for love, for this sense of defenselessness against pain and heartbreak was unnerving.

So, now what? he asked himself. He'd thank her for a nice time and send her on her way? That was lousy, really lousy. No, he'd ease out of her life slowly so she had time to adjust, and then he'd never see her again.

He frowned. Never see her again? he repeated. Well, it would be better that way. He'd get his life

back on track and go about his business. Without
Tricia. Without her smile and laughter, the sweet
nectar of her kisses, the warm haven of her body.
Right. That was how it would be, because he just
didn't want to be in love now.

A restlessness swept through him, a wired energy that made it impossible for him to lie quietly.
He carefully edged away from Tricia, then waited
to see if she would awaken. She murmured his
name but did not open her eyes. He took another
quick shower, then dressed in jeans and a knit
shirt. He'd make dinner, such as it was, he decided.

When he returned to the bedroom carrying a
tray, Tricia was still sleeping. He gazed down at
her and his heart did a strange tap dance when
he saw that she was hugging his pillow.

He set the tray on the nightstand. How did
Tricia feel about *him*? he wondered suddenly. Not
that it mattered, but did she love him at all? It
didn't make any difference one way or another,
but surely she hadn't given herself to him solely
because she liked his looks or had decided he'd be
a good lover. No, Tricia wouldn't do that. Would
she? He really didn't care, but wasn't she even a
little in love with him?

"Knock it off, Walker," he muttered. "It's no big
deal. But still . . . No, forget it. You're really losing
it."

He sat down on the edge of the bed and gently
shook her shoulder. "Tricia? Tricia, wake up. I
made us something to eat."

"Hmm?" She slowly opened her eyes. "What?"

"Dinner," he said, gesturing toward the tray.

"Oh, how nice." She yawned, then stretched

like a lazy kitten. The sheet slipped below her breasts, and Spence groaned silently. "I'm hungry."

"Yeah," he said, tearing his gaze from her breasts. "Me too. Prop up there and I'll put this tray across your legs."

She scooted up, pushing the pillows behind her, then tugged the sheet up and tucked it under her arms. Spence set the tray across her thighs.

"Tomato soup and grilled cheese sandwiches," he said, picking up a mug of soup. "And, no, that's not homemade bread."

She laughed and bit into a sandwich. They ate in silence for several minutes.

"You have an awful frown on your face, Spence," Tricia said finally. "Is something wrong?"

"No," he said, staring into his mug.

"I guess when I promised you I wouldn't be sorry we made love, I should have asked for the same promise from you."

His head snapped up and he looked at her, still frowning.

"I'm not sorry," he said. "What man would be, after sharing what we did? It's just that I feel you picked the wrong man."

"I'm not asking for anything, Spence."

"Well, dammit, you should be," he said, his voice rising. "I should have left you alone the moment I realized you were a virgin. But not me, not hot-shot Walker. I wanted you. Damn, how I wanted you."

"And I wanted you. For someone who claims he isn't sorry we made love, you certainly don't sound very happy about it."

"You don't understand," he said. He'd fallen in love with her, dammit!

"No, I guess I don't." She pushed her sandwich back and forth on the plate. "I made a decision regarding my life, my body, and I have every right to do that. What we shared we did by mutual consent, which is how it should be. I made it clear that I don't expect any commitment or promise from you."

"Oh, is that so?" he said, setting his mug back on the tray with a loud clunk. "What's next? You go try out your new talents on the next guy who strikes your fancy? What was this?" He swept his arm in the air over the bed. "Basic training?"

"How dare you say such a thing!"

"If you don't expect commitment or promises," he said, lunging to his feet, "aren't you also saying you don't intend to make any?"

"We're not talking about me, Spence Walker. You're the one going on and on about not being ready for a commitment. But just for the record, what I do when you ride off into the sunset is none of your damn business."

"The hell it isn't, lady. And don't swear."

"I'll swear whenever I feel like it," she said. "Dammit," she added as an afterthought. "This conversation isn't making one bit of sense. I made love with you knowing we have no future together. What are you ranting and raving about? If you have some misplaced sense of guilt or responsibility because you were my first lover, you can just forget it. I knew exactly what I was doing and I'm not sorry." She took a bite of her sandwich and glared at him while she chewed.

"I don't want you with anyone else," he said, looking down at her from an intimidating height. "No one touches you but me."

She sniffed indignantly. "I will do whatever I please, Lieutenant."

"Don't push me, Tricia."

"You don't scare me," she said, and licked a blob of cheese off the end of her finger.

"Hell," he said, and stalked across the room. He leaned his shoulder against the wall and glowered at the ceiling. Easy, Walker, he told himself. He was coming unglued, carrying on like a blithering idiot.

What in hell was he going to do? he wondered. He loved her. He didn't want to love her. He didn't want anyone else to love her. Wonderful. He needed to think this through, but that was impossible while Tricia was sitting there with her enticing body covered by nothing but a sheet. She was getting sassy, too, all spit and fire. Lord, she was something. And he loved her.

"Okay," he said, and took a deep breath as he pushed himself away from the wall. "I think we'll give this discussion a rest, since it's only going in circles. We'll take one day at a time. Let's leave it at that for now."

"Fine," she said. "Thank you for the dinner. I'll go see if my clothes are dry."

"They're not. I took another shower and steamed up the bathroom."

"Oh."

"You could stay here tonight," he suggested, walking slowly toward the bed.

"Here?"

"Yeah." He sat down next to her. "I'd like you to stay."

"You would?" she asked, smiling.

He nodded. "I would." He leaned forward to kiss her. "Okay?" he asked when he lifted his head.

"Okay."

"I'll get this tray out of your way."

"I think I'll go take a shower."

As Spence left the room with the tray, Tricia slipped off the bed, snatched the robe from the floor, and dashed to the bathroom. Her body definitely complained at her sudden movements, and she welcomed the soothing warm water of the shower. The slight discomfort in foreign places of her body did not distress her, but was evidence of the exquisite lovemaking she'd shared with Spence.

That man wasn't exactly making sense, she mused. He didn't want a permanent relationship with her, but bellowed in anger at the thought of her being with another man. Was that how macho types always behaved? She didn't know. All the men she knew leaned more toward wimpy.

"If I didn't know better," she said to the shower nozzle, "I'd think the man was falling in love with me." She sighed. "Quit dreaming, Patricia. Just quit dreaming."

Six

Tricia emerged from the steamy bathroom clad again in the huge bathrobe. She found two rubber bands in her bag and they held the sleeves snugly at her wrists. After treating herself to a butterscotch ball, she walked into the living room. Spence was slouched on the sofa, watching television.

She stood still for a moment and stared at him. At his long, muscular legs stretched out in front of him and crossed at the ankle. At his broad chest and wide shoulders, his handsome face. She adored, absolutely adored, his thick sun-streaked hair. He was rough-edged and earthy. He was a man. He was Spence. And she loved him.

"What are you watching?" she asked.

He turned his head to look at her.

"You," he said, and extended his hand to her. "Come here."

She placed her hand in his, and he pulled her down next to him.

"How are you?" he asked, circling her shoulders with his arm.

"Wonderful."

"I'm serious, Tricia. I know I hurt you when we made love, and I need to know if you're all right."

"Yes, I'm really all right."

"Well, when we go to bed later, I'm just going to hold you in my arms. You've had enough of me being all over you for one night."

"Don't I get to have an opinion on the subject?"

"No. Give yourself a chance to recuperate a bit. There will be other times to make love."

She leaned her head on his shoulder. "Will there?"

"That's a dumb question. Just having you near me like this makes me want you."

"I want you, too, Spence."

"Change the subject. It's going to be a long enough night as it is with you curled up next to me. It'll either do wonders for my character or cause me to break out in hives. Watch the movie. I have no idea what it is, but watch it anyway."

"Spence?"

"Yeah?"

"I love you."

Every muscle in his body seemed to tense, and she felt as though she were leaning against a concrete wall. She lifted her head to look up at him. His eyes were wide, his expression stunned.

"What?" he said.

"I love you. I realize that doesn't change anything, but I thought you should know. I couldn't bear it if you came to the conclusion that I had made love with you out of a sense of curiosity or some such thing. I made love with you because I love you. I know you don't want to be loved, but it really doesn't concern you, anyway. It's mine to deal with. I'm only telling you so you'll understand why I decided to do what I did. My mind was made up, Spence. You mustn't feel any guilt or responsibility toward me. End of story." She plopped her head back onto his shoulder.

She loved him? Spence thought, dazed. What was she using for brains, oatmeal? She had no business falling in love with him. Of course, he shouldn't have fallen in love with her either. Good Lord, she loved him. This was the most fantastic, unbelievable, glorious— This was terrible!

Her head popped back up.

"What's wrong?" he asked.

"Your muscles are twitching. You're bouncing my head around. Relax, Spence. I don't expect you to respond to what I just said."

"You shouldn't love me, Tricia," he said gruffly. "I thought you had better sense than that."

"Well, for heaven's sake, I didn't do it on purpose. It just happened. A person doesn't have any control over this type of emotion."

Tell me about it, he thought dismally.

"Forget I mentioned it," she said.

"Oh, right," he said dryly. "I'll erase it from my memory bank."

"I'm sure I'm not the first woman to declare her love for you."

"No."

"Figures. Don't tell me how many there have

been. I'll feel like I'm in line at the bakery. Maybe I shouldn't have told you. I just wanted to be totally honest about it."

"I'm glad you told me. Or at least I think I'm glad. Hell, I don't know. My brain is turning into scrambled eggs."

"You poor dear," she said, patting his knee. "Let's talk about something else."

"Such as?"

She smiled brightly. "Freddy."

Spence moaned, dropping his face into his hands. "Give me strength. Why would I want to talk about that scum?"

"He's not a scum! He's a young boy who has taken up with the wrong crowd and needs a new sense of direction. The judge knew that. You said yourself that Freddy was ordered to stay away from the street gang. The fact that he's to get counseling proves they're aware that he needs some help discovering his own identity."

"This is all very fascinating," Spence said, "but what does it have to do with me, or you, for that matter?"

"I just wish you would be a little more open-minded about Freddy, that's all."

"Why?"

"Why?" she repeated.

"Yeah, why? That's your favorite question. You answer it for a change. Why should I do a one-eighty about Freddy?"

"Because I . . . because . . . because it would be nice if you did," she said lamely. Oh, darn, she thought. That hadn't gone well at all.

"I've seen a hundred Freddys," he said. "Granted,

his was the first juvenile case I've been involved in, as my department usually gets them when they've hit the big time. But that's where he's headed. Counseling and orders to stay away from that gang aren't going to stop him."

She was going to stop him, Tricia thought fiercely. Okay, she'd tried to bring up the subject of Freddy, but Spence obviously wasn't interested in listening to reason. She'd just have to show him that Freddy was a worthwhile human being. And she would. Later. After she'd shaped Freddy up and straightened out his attitude. She really had a lot of work to do on that boy's attitude.

"Did you know that Frederick means 'peaceful chieftain'?" she asked.

Spence hooted with laughter. "No joke? He may be the chief of his own gang someday, but there will be nothing peaceful about him and his cronies."

"Forget it," Tricia said, glaring at him. "Change the subject."

"Again?" Spence asked, still smiling. The telephone rang and he picked up the receiver. "Walker . . . yeah, Ted . . . He did? . . . Yeah, finally. I'm on my way." He slammed down the receiver and got to his feet in the same motion.

"Trouble?" Tricia asked.

"A key figure in a burglary ring has surfaced after disappearing for weeks. We've been waiting for this. I've got to go, Tricia. You wait here, okay? I'm not sure when I'll get back. Go on to bed if you get tired."

"Okay," she said.

He pulled her up into his arms. "I don't want to leave you. Will you be all right here alone?"

"Of course. I'll be waiting for you."

"That sounds very nice."

He kissed her, and again desire rose within Tricia. When her knees began to tremble, she clung to his shoulders for support.

At last he gently set her away from him.

"Hold that thought," he said. She could do no more than bob her head in agreement. He grabbed his gun and jacket and left the apartment.

" 'Bye," she said to the empty room. She sank onto the sofa as her wobbly legs refused to hold her, and pressed her hand to her forehead. "Mercy, that man's kisses are potent."

She drew her legs up, wrapped her arms around them, and rested her chin on her knees. Her mind replayed the events of the evening—the indescribable beauty of the lovemaking with Spence, her declaration of love, all the things that Spence had said and done.

She smiled as a warm glow spread throughout her. Spence cared for her, she just knew he did. So, okay, he hadn't said that he loved her, but he did care for her. The mere mention of her being with another man had produced a raging fury in him and enough yelling to crack the plaster. A man didn't yell like that unless he cared.

So, now what? she asked herself. She was racing against some invisible clock inside Spence. He could very well have an internal alarm that would ring when he'd been in a relationship too long, when it was beginning to hint at commitment. She had to figure out how to change his "caring for her" into "falling in love with her" before that buzzer went off. Oh, really? How did one go about doing that?

She gazed absently at the television, then paid more attention as a woman on the screen began seducing a man.

"There's one idea," she said aloud.

She fluttered her eyelashes and slipped the robe back to reveal her bare shoulders. In an exaggerated version of a bump and grind, she inched the robe lower as she rotated her hips.

" 'Cause I'm a wo—" she began to sing, then dissolved into laughter and fell back onto the sofa. "Have a butterscotch ball, Tricia," she said, gasping for air. "You'll feel better."

At midnight she crawled into Spence's bed with every intention of staying awake until he returned. Two long, noisy yawns later, she fell asleep.

The next thing Tricia knew the warmth of the early morning sun was tiptoeing across her face. Her eyes popped open, and she wondered for a moment where she was.

Spence, she thought, turning her head on the pillow. No Spence. Had he been out all night dealing with that crummy crook? Freddy certainly didn't cause those kinds of problems. Well, he wouldn't from now on, anyway. She hoped.

"Freddy," she said, sitting bolt upright. She was meeting him at a diner near her office building at eight o'clock to hear a report on his job-seeking project. She had to call a taxi, get home, change her clothes. And she needed to see Spence. "Darn," she said, slipping off the bed. "Some morning-after this is."

She dressed in her stiff, dry clothes, phoned for a taxi, then with a wistful smile on her face stood at the bedroom door and gazed at the rumpled bed.

"I love you, Spence," she whispered, then turned and hurried from the apartment.

Freddy slid into the seat across from Tricia at the diner and scowled at her.

"Good morning," she said cheerfully. "Would you like some breakfast?"

"No. My mom fixes breakfast before she goes to work."

"No, thank you."

"Huh?"

"When you refuse an offer, Freddy, you say, 'no, thank you.' "

He rolled his eyes. "No, thank you, ma'am, I've already eaten. There, how's that?"

"Splendid. So, how did it go with the job hunting?"

"Nothing. Not a damn thing. They wouldn't even take my application at the car wash. I'm telling you, Miss . . . um . . ."

"Tricia."

"Tricia, there's nothing out there."

"Yes, there is," she said, leaning toward him. "You can't give up. This may sound rude, Freddy, but what did you wear when you applied for those jobs?"

"This," he said, glancing down at his T-shirt

and jeans. "Your fancy haircut sure didn't help any."

"Did it ever occur to you that wearing a t-shirt with the slogan 'you can take this job and shove it' on it might turn prospective employers off?"

"Oh." He peered at his shirt again. "I didn't mean anything personal by it. It was the only shirt I had that was clean. You didn't tell Walker that you're reforming me, did you?"

"No. Why?"

"Because the longer we sneak around behind his back the better. He'll blow a gasket when he finds out how long his lady has been conning him." He rubbed his hands together. "I love it, I love it."

"Oh, put a cork in it," Tricia said, glaring at him. He blinked in surprise. "I realize you and I have different reasons for reforming you, Freddy, but I don't want to hear one more word about how we're conning Lieutenant Walker. Is that clear?"

"Yeah, sure, fine. Don't get hyper."

"Now then, I want to ask you something."

"Fire away."

"Freddy," she said, her tone gentling, "do you have a dream? A wish? A fantasy deep inside you of what you've always wanted to be?"

For just a moment she saw a vulnerability in his eyes, saw his tough-guy façade slip before he shrugged and stared out the window.

"Naw," he said.

"Freddy, look at me." He turned his head slowly to meet her gaze. "When I was growing up, I was a disaster. I was so disorganized I nearly flunked out of school. I'd do my homework, then forget where I put it, and wouldn't have it to turn in. After my father died, my sister and I got baby-sitting jobs. Later, we worked part-time to help out."

"I thought you said you had everything you needed."

"We did. My father's insurance paid off the mortgage on the house, so we had a lovely home. My mother got a job for the first time in twenty years. Kathy, my sister, and I earned money for our clothes. We didn't have a lot of extras, but we did all right. What I didn't have, Freddy, was self-esteem, confidence in myself, because I messed up everything I did."

"Yeah, I know the feeling," he said, fiddling with a spoon. "I guess you outgrew your screwing-up stage, huh?"

She laughed. "No, I didn't. I'm still so disorganized it's ridiculous. I've had to accept that about myself. But, Freddy, I found my place, realized my dream. Math, numbers. I'm a CPA, and I'm so good at it, I'm awesome. I have my own business in that building where we . . . um, met."

"Not bad," he said.

"Freddy," she said softly, touching his hand, "do you have a dream, a place where you know you belong?"

She was hardly breathing as she watched Freddy struggle with himself over whether he should confide in her.

"I—" he started, then took a deep breath. "I want . . . I want to be a chef."

"A chef?" she said eagerly. "Really?"

"Forget it," he said, yanking his hand away. He folded his arms across his chest and glowered at the napkin holder. "Just forget it."

"Can you cook?"

He snapped his head around to look at her. "Damn right, I can. I took home ec. in school 'cause I needed one more credit to graduate. The guys hassled me about it till I busted a few faces. But when I got in that class, I blew their minds. I make a soufflé that you wouldn't believe. My pie crust is so flaky it just about floats out of the pan. Know what? The teacher hired me, paid me money, to make some quiches for a party she was having. Yeah, being a chef, that's my dream. Now, go ahead and laugh your head off, I don't care."

"I never laugh at dreams," Tricia said quietly. "Thank you for telling me, Freddy. There has to be a way to make your dream come true."

"Not a chance."

"Well, I'll think about it. Listen, I have to get to work. Meet me in the parking lot of my office building at five-thirty."

"Why?"

"Because we're going shopping for clothes for you. The next time you apply for a job, you're going to look presentable."

"Clothes cost money."

"I'll put it on your tab," she said, smiling. "You can pay me back when you become Chef Jackson."

"Tricia, you're bonkers."

"I believe the term is ba-nan-as," she said merrily as she slid out of the booth. "See you later, Freddy."

• • •

Spence was sitting on the steps of Tricia's house. He glanced at the woods, then shifted his gaze to the sky. The sun looked like a melting scoop of butter as it set, changing the white clouds to vibrant shades of red and orange and purple. Even the green leaves of the trees seemed to shimmer with glorious color.

There was a sense of serenity here, Spence mused. A gentleness. This was a special place, Tricia's place. And he missed her.

It had been nearly noon before he had returned to his apartment. His exhaustion had been numbing, and he'd flung himself across the bed and slept the afternoon away. When he awoke, he'd showered, shaved, dressed in clean jeans and a black knit shirt, and eaten a huge lunch.

And through it all, he'd thought of Tricia.

He'd wandered aimlessly through the apartment, and in his mind he'd seen her face, heard her laughter. He had remembered the exquisite pleasure of their lovemaking and decided it had been really lousy that he'd had to leave her last night. Nice guy that he was, he'd surprise her by dropping in to see her, to make sure she wasn't upset about anything that had happened. Yeah, he'd go see her. For her sake, of course.

Now here he sat on her front step watching a sunset that was rapidly losing its charm. Where in hell was she? Working hours were long since over, he knew she still had gas in her car, so where was she? He'd sure as hell be glad when he wasn't in love with her anymore because, he was quickly discovering, worrying about her caused a painful knot in his gut. Dammit, where was she?

• • •

As Tricia drove home, she added in her mind the cost of the clothes she had purchased for Freddy and grimaced at the total. Oh, well, she thought, it was money well spent. In slacks and dress shirts, Freddy was going to make a much better impression when he applied for work.

A chef, she mused. That was about the last thing she would have ever imagined as being Freddy's secret dream. There had to be a way to make it come true. There just had to be.

She turned onto her street and as she neared her house she saw Spence's car.

"Uh-oh," she said. "Where have I been? Think, Tricia! Where have you been?"

She pulled into her driveway and got out of the car. As she slammed the door shut, she wished she had a butterscotch ball. Plastering a smile on her face, she started toward the house. Spence stood up. He definitely wasn't smiling.

"Uh-oh," she muttered again. "Hi," she said when she reached him. "This is a surprise. A nice surprise, of course, but still a surprise. I wasn't expecting you, but I'm delighted you're here. So, Spence, how's life?"

He frowned. "Care to join me?" he asked, indicating the step with a sweeping gesture.

"Great," she said, and sat down. "We can watch the sunset together. Super."

He settled next to her, resting his elbows on his knees and lacing his fingers loosely together. He looked up at the still glorious sky.

"I was worried about you," he said, his voice low.

"I'm sorry. But, Spence, I really didn't expect you to be here, so there was no reason for me to rush home. I apologize for any concern I caused you." He cared, he cared, he cared! her heart sang.

"Yeah, okay," he said, sighing. "I'm off base, anyway. You had no way of knowing I was here. But why are you so late?"

"Errands. I had errands to run. Isn't this sunset marvelous?"

"Yeah, I can't remember when I last sat still long enough to appreciate one."

A silence fell. Neither spoke as they watched nature's paintbrush work its magic in the heavens. Crickets began their serenade. A rabbit appeared, then dashed away. An orange haze seemed to sift down from the sky, transforming all it dusted until they were enveloped in a peaceful glow of soft color.

Then slowly the tranquility changed as Tricia became acutely conscious of Spence, and he of her. A tension, heavy with sensuality, wove back and forth between them. Their heartbeats quickened, and at the same moment, as if in response to an unspoken message, they turned to look at each other. Their gazes held for a moment, then Spence kissed her, a kiss that was as gentle as the oncoming night.

Tricia's eyes drifted closed as she savored the feeling of Spence's mouth on hers. His tongue slid along her teeth, then slipped inside. Their arms wrapped around each other, and the kiss deepened.

Her soft whimper was matched by his groan as their passions were kindled to a roaring flame. The kiss became urgent, frenzied, almost rough.

They needed. They wanted. Their hearts thundered, and blood pounded in their veins.

The night became a cloak, its darkness shielding them from all that was beyond them. It wrapped around them, creating a private space for only the two of them and the sounds of nature.

"I want you, Tricia," Spence murmured.

"Yes. Yes, I want you, too."

"Come inside the house with me. Let me love you."

"Yes," she whispered, and placed her hand in his.

In the bedroom he pulled her into his arms and kissed her until she was clutching at him, her body humming with desire. His breathing was ragged as he reached for the buttons on her blouse.

Moments later she stood naked before him, trembling as his hot gaze raked over her. He quickly shed his clothes, then led her to the bed. He stretched out next to her, propping himself on his elbow.

"You're beautiful," he said, palming one of her breasts. "We're wonderful together, just so damn good."

"Yes" was all she managed to say.

As his tongue delved deep into her mouth, his hand roamed over her silken skin to the heated place he sought. Her soft moan as he caressed her sent his passion soaring. He shifted to seek her breast with his mouth, but at that moment she pushed gently against his chest, urging him to roll over onto his back.

"My turn," she said, her voice husky with desire. "I'll tend to your needs."

With feathery kisses she began a languorous journey, exploring every inch of him. His arms fell to his sides, his hands curled into fists as he struggled for control.

"Lord," he muttered. "You're . . . unbelievable. Tricia, I can't take too much of this. You won't be ready for me."

"I'll be ready," she said. "Do you like this, Spence?"

"Oh, yes, yes . . ."

With tongue and teeth and lips and hands she worked her magic until his breathing was rough and his body glistened with perspiration.

"No more," he growled.

He grabbed her waist and rolled her over beneath him. In the next instant he entered her with a thrust that seemed to steal the breath from her body.

"Yes," she gasped. "Oh, yes."

She matched his pounding rhythm, lifting her hips to bring him closer, to fill her, consume her. Their thundering movements carried them away into a roaring, spiraling maze of sensations.

"Tricia!"

The shudderings of his body matched the ecstasy sweeping through hers. They were hurled into oblivion and drifted back slowly.

Spence lifted himself off her and lay on his side, then pulled her close, wrapping his arm around her beneath her breasts. "That was incredible," he said. "Where did you learn . . . that's dumb. You just instinctively knew how to give me pleasure, how to be one helluva woman. You're really something."

"Only for you."

"Did I hurt you, Tricia? I was so damn rough."

"Oh, no, it was wonderful. I'm glad I pleased you, Spence."

"That's putting it mildly."

She snuggled closer to him. "I should think about fixing dinner."

"We'll send out for Chinese . . . later," he said, weaving his fingers through her curls. "Your hair is like silk."

"Spence, if you wanted to be a chef, what would you do?"

"Fail miserably. I can cook about three or four things, all of which are barely edible."

"No, I mean, if a person had a dream to be a chef, what would they do?"

"Go to chef school, I suppose. Your hair smells like flowers."

"Yes, of course, a school. Why didn't I think of that?"

"Changing careers, are you? Your skin is so soft." He trailed his fingers down her arm, then gently stroked her breast.

"No, I'm not changing my— Oh!" She gasped as his thumb flicked across her nipple.

"Who wants to be a chef?" he asked, slowly lowering his lips toward hers.

"A who?"

"Chef."

"I have no idea," she said dreamily. "Oh, kiss me, Spence, before I go ba-nan-as."

"I intend to. I intend to kiss you for a long, long time."

And he did. Again they left reality behind to find

the treasured place known only to them when they were one. It was ecstasy.

Much, much later, Spence pulled on his jeans and phoned in an order for Chinese food. When the multitude of little white boxes were delivered, they ate their fill, then watched, to Tricia's delight, an old Humphrey Bogart movie on television.

"I should be going," Spence said when the movie ended.

"Stay," she whispered.

"Sold."

He scooped her into his arms and carried her into the bedroom, where they made love far into the night. When Tricia was deeply asleep, tucked close to Spence's side, he closed his eyes in sated contentment. His last conscious thought was the realization that Tricia had never answered his question.

Who wanted to be a chef?

Seven

"Tricia, please," Freddy said, moaning as he sank onto her sofa. "Give me a break. I can't think anymore." He leaned his head back and closed his eyes. "My brain is mush."

Tricia looked up at him from where she sat Indian style on the floor, a large book propped across her lap.

"You can't quit yet," she said. "You've got to study if you hope to have any chance at all for that scholarship to the chef school. The exam is in two weeks. Freddy, sit up, you're slouching. It's important that you stand up straight when you stand, and sit up straight when you sit. Now, then, what is café au lait?"

Freddy groaned.

"Café au lait."

"Coffee with hot milk. Tricia, when is Walker getting back from Colorado Springs?"

She frowned. "I've explained it to you twice already. Please, sit up. What is macedoine?"

He wiggled to an upright position. "A mixture of fruits or vegetables. Tell me Walker's schedule again. It wouldn't do for him to catch me here, you know."

She sighed. "Spence came by my office on Thursday to say he'd been called to testify at a trial that had gotten a change of venue to Colorado Springs. He left." After kissing her senseless, she mentally tacked on. Mercy! "He doesn't expect to get back until very late on Monday." She missed him. Dear heaven, how she missed him. He'd phoned her both Thursday and Friday nights, but it just wasn't the same as having him with her. "Got that?"

"Yeah. Then you called the French dude at the chef school and found out scholarships are available, and we've been dissolving my brain ever since. It's Saturday night, Tricia. Have a heart. Can't we lighten up?"

"No. What's a ramekin?"

"An individual baking dish."

"Good. Oh, Freddy, you're doing wonderfully. I can't believe how fast you're learning all this. And that dinner you made us was fantastic." They had had stuffed pork chops with apple rings, asparagus spears, tomatoes vinaigrette, and blueberry pie.

"*I* thought so," he said smugly. "Outstanding."

"It certainly was. You have a natural talent for cooking, and for making everything so attractive when you serve it. You're going to be a top-notch chef."

"Only if I get a scholarship to that fancy school," he said, frowning. "They sure want big bucks to go there."

"And you'll get the scholarship if you study. Sit up straight. You're slouching again. What is pâté de foie gras?"

"Goose liver paste. Gross. I need to stretch my legs." He stood up. "I start my job at the movie theater Monday afternoon, you know. Just what I always wanted to do; clean up other peoples' grungy popcorn off the floor."

"It won't be forever," she said, watching him wander around the room. "You have a chance at a future, at seeing your dream come true."

He shrugged. "Maybe. I've learned not to count on anything. That way, I don't get uptight when it doesn't happen. Why are your plants sitting on the floor next to the ceramic pots? Is this a new way to decorate?"

"No." She sighed. "Two young boys broke in here and ransacked the place. I bought those plants and pots to replace the ones they smashed. I just haven't had time to transplant them yet."

He stared at her, his jaw tight. "Punks trashed this place, Tricia? When?"

"The same day I . . . met you on the stairs of the office building."

"Damn. Who were they? I'll make sure they never come near you again, Tricia. Never. You shouldn't be living in this place, you know. It's too isolated, and those woods are a perfect screen for anyone to sneak up on you. Walker must be nuts letting you live here. Give me the names of the yo-yos who broke in here. I'll take care of them."

Tricia scrambled to her feet and planted her hands on her hips. "You'll do no such thing, Freddy Jackson. I wouldn't give you their names if I knew them. You're on probation, remember? And, for your information, no one tells me where I may or may not live."

"Man, oh, man," Freddy said, shaking his head. "Walker sure has his hands full with you."

"I thought you planned to be a chef, not a chauvinist. Enough of this. Let's get back to work. You've got to know this stuff forward and backward before the exam."

"Yeah, I know. Okay, we study, but I need a break. How about I help you fix up these plants?"

"Well . . ."

"Good. What do we do first?"

"All right, you win. We'll tend to the plants then—" The ringing of the phone interrupted her and she snatched up the receiver. "Hello?"

"Tricia? Spence."

"Spence?" she said, glancing quickly at Freddy. "You're calling earlier than you did the last two nights."

"Is that a problem?"

"No. No, of course, not." She watched Freddy pick up a creeping Charlie. "How is it going there?"

"The same. I'm holed up with the D.A. going over every little detail before I testify on Monday. It's boring as hell but necessary. This trial has been postponed three times before they went for the change of venue. The whole thing went down with this joker months ago, and I have to review, get my facts straight."

"Studying can be tedious," she said. Freddy rolled his eyes heavenward and nodded. "But you'll still be home Monday night?"

"I don't see why not. I go on the stand early Monday. Tricia, I . . . well, I miss you."

"Oh, how nice," she said with a sigh. "I miss you too, Spence." Freddy crossed his eyes and made a face. She glared at him.

"So, what are you doing tonight to keep busy?" Spence asked.

"Doing? Tonight? Oh, well, I'm about to transplant my plants into the new pots. Yes-sir-ee, that's what I'm doing, all right. Fun, huh?"

"Blows my mind," Spence said, laughing. "Well, recess is over. I guess I'd better get back to work. The D.A. is waiting for me in his room. He's a real slave driver."

"I'm so glad you called," she said. She watched as Freddy peered closely at her creeping Charlie, one of its leaves tickling his nose. "Sleep well."

"I'd sleep better if you were next to me."

"Oh, well, I . . . oh." A warm flush rushed to her face. "Yes. Well."

Spence chuckled.

And Freddy Jackson sneezed.

Tricia nearly dropped the phone as she spun around in wide-eyed horror. Freddy shrugged his apology, a helpless expression on his face. He set the plant on the floor and raised his hands in a gesture of peace, then clasped them together in an imitation of prayer.

"Tricia," a deep, menacing voice said in her ear.

"Yes?" she squeaked.

"Who sneezed?"

Spence was clenching his jaw, she thought frantically. That was his clenching-his-jaw voice. Oh, dear Lord, what was she going to say? "Cat," she blurted out. "You know, that ugly cat who thinks he lives here, but he doesn't, but I feed him, so he keeps coming around? That cat. Yep. That was Ugly the Cat who sneezed. He's allergic to my plants, I guess. Well, Spence, it was really superduper talking to you, but I'm busy as a bee. Talk to you tomorrow, okay? You bet. 'Bye." She slammed down the receiver.

"Tricia, I—" Freddy started.

"Aaagh!" she screamed. "I'm going to strangle you with my bare hands!"

"Stay calm," he said, taking a step backward.

"Don't speak to me," she said, and stomped past him into the kitchen. She yanked open the cupboard and reached for a bag of butterscotch balls. After tearing off the wrappers, she stuffed six of the candies into her mouth and returned to the living room.

"What's wrong with your face?" Freddy asked.

"Nuffing," she mumbled.

"Your cheeks are swollen or something. What did you do out there in the kitchen?"

"Bubberbotchballs," she said, shifting them around in her mouth. "Heps ma nerbes."

"Helps your nerves?"

"Mmm." She crunched noisily on the candy as Freddy eyed her warily. She swallowed, then drew a steadying breath. "There. That's better."

"Thank God," he said.

"Aaagh!" she screamed.

He flattened himself against the door.

Spence stared at the telephone in his motel room with narrowed eyes. One message hammered in his brain: There was a man in Tricia's cottage!

"Dammit!" he said. He got to his feet and began to pace the small room with heavy, thudding steps. Tricia was with another man. That sneeze hadn't come from any damn cat. Did she think he was stupid? She was two-timing him. The minute he left town she found a replacement for him. What happened to her being in love with him? She was with another man!

And it hurt like hell.

Spence stopped and ran his hand down his face, drawing in a shuddering breath. The image in his mind of Tricia in the arms of The Sneezer caused a knot to coil painfully in his gut, coupled with cold fury—and a dark emptiness.

What did he expect? his little voice whispered. He'd made it clear to Tricia that he wasn't ready for a commitment. He'd known all along she wasn't cut out for a brief affair, that she needed security, the assurance of a future with one special man.

"With me!" he said, thumping himself on the chest. He was going to take The Sneezer apart limb by limb. Tricia was Spence Walker's woman, by damn, and no one, *no one*, touched her but him. He'd make that very clear to her and the sleazeballs of Denver when he married Tricia and put *his* ring on her finger.

"When I do what?" he said aloud, sinking onto the edge of the bed.

Marry Tricia? his mind echoed. Now? Be a husband, then a father? That would mean staying in love, not allowing the emotion to evaporate as he'd planned. That would mean making love to Tricia every night and waking up next to her every morning. When he came home worn and weary, she would be there with her sunshine smile to make him whole again. Oh, yes, he did love that woman.

But love was so damn big and powerful, so all-consuming. There he sat, tough-cop Walker, scared to death to open his mouth and say the words that would commit him to Tricia for the rest of his life.

He'd been playing mind games, he admitted. The timing of Tricia's emergence into his life wasn't wrong. It was love itself that had him shaking in his shoes.

"Hell," he muttered. "What am I going to do?"

You're going to lose Tricia, his little voice whispered.

No! he shouted silently. He couldn't, wouldn't, allow that to happen. But he needed some time, he had to think this through.

What about The Sneezer? the voice asked tauntingly. Tricia was with The Sneezer.

"I'll murder him," Spence said, lunging to his feet.

The telephone rang, and he spun around so fast he knocked the receiver onto the floor. He snatched it up.

"Yeah?"

"Spence?" the district attorney said. "Are you coming? We've still got a lot of material to cover here to be ready for Monday."

"Yeah. I'm on my way."

Frowning ferociously, Spence strode from the room.

At midnight Tricia crawled wearily into bed. She sighed as she replayed in her mind the telephone conversation with Spence.

"Oh-h-h," she moaned, "why, why, why did Freddy have to sneeze?" It hadn't been his fault. She knew that and had told him as much. He'd apologized fifteen times, saying he hadn't meant to sneeze, but the creeping Charlie had tickled his nose.

She had assumed that Freddy simply didn't want to disrupt his plan to put one over on Spence by being secretly reformed by her. But he had said, "I'm really sorry, Tricia. You look like you're going to cry. Damn, I wouldn't do anything to make you cry." At that moment she had known she had not been wrong to put her faith in Freddy Jackson.

But, she thought, staring up into the darkness, that did not erase the sneeze, nor the fact that she had literally hung up on Spence. The man was not an idiot. There hadn't been a cat created that could sneeze like that.

"Spence thinks I was with another man," she said to the night. "Lordy, what a mess." Or was it? Slowly, an idea began forming in her mind.

When alone in Spence's apartment she had vowed to fight for his love, even though she didn't know how. What if Spence thought he had competition, that she was becoming dissatisfied with his lack of commitment and was looking elsewhere?

"Risky," she said aloud. "Very risky." Spence could blow a gasket and walk out of her life without a backward glance. But his leaving was already guaranteed, her heartache a sure thing. This way, she would have at least tried *something* to win his love.

It was a crummy plan, she admitted, but it was all she had. She would view Freddy's sneeze as an act of fate, and go with it. She'd let the chips fall where they may, and hope that among them weren't the pieces of her shattered heart.

Freddy arrived at Tricia's early Sunday as promised. The morning was spent in intense studying, and Tricia was once again impressed with Freddy's total recall of what he'd read in the textbook. At noon he pleaded for a break, and prepared star-shaped ham sandwiches for their lunch.

"The Marines could use you," he said as they ate. "You're a tough drill sergeant, Tricia."

"Me? Get your elbows off the table."

"What do my elbows have to do with me being a chef?"

"We're working on your total person. It's important that you have social graces, know how to dress and act, no matter what situation you may find yourself in."

"You're driving me crazy," he said, shaking his head. "Do you know that at breakfast I said, 'May I have the salt, please?' and my sisters stared at me like they'd never seen me before?"

"That's splendid," Tricia said.

"It's embarrassing. Can't you lighten up? Just concentrate on the chef jazz?"

"Absolutely not. Freddy, your elbows."

"I can't take much more of this," he muttered. "I'm going right out of my tree."

Tricia heard him, but ignored his complaints. They ate in silence for several minutes, and she wondered what Spence was thinking about the man who had sneezed. No, she decided, she'd better push all that from her mind for now and concentrate on Freddy and his elbows.

"Why did you get mixed up with that street gang, Freddy?" she asked.

He shrugged. "I don't know. I was bummed out. I got laid off from the grocery store and couldn't find another job. I was tired of the whole scene, I guess. There's never enough money, my mom works so damn hard, my sisters don't have nice clothes to wear. I just freaked for a while. I was only with those jerks for a couple of weeks."

"You haven't been near them since the judge put you on probation, have you?"

"Just once to tell them I wasn't joining up. I made it sound like if I got hauled in again they'd go with me. They're not hassling me."

"Good."

"You know, Tricia, I've been thinking. I can tell you're really hung up on Walker, and he's liable to hit the roof when he finds out you're messing around with reforming me. It might be better if I just studied on my own for the exam."

"Absolutely not," she said, shaking her head. "Besides, the exam is only part of it. We're working on your total person, remember? Get your elbows off the table."

"But you're driving me crazy!"

"Hush. And don't you dare swear. That's next on the agenda. We're going to clean up your mouth."

"Ah, hell."

A thoroughly exhausted Freddy left the cottage at six o'clock, and Tricia immediately turned to stare at the telephone.

Would Spence call? she wondered frantically. What if he came right out and asked her about the man who had sneezed? She was such a lousy liar. She was liable to blurt out the truth about Freddy. Oh, heaven forbid.

When the telephone rang at eight o'clock, she jumped, then forced herself to count to five before she answered it.

"Patricia Todd here," she said, wondering if she sounded like Princess Di.

"Spencer Walker here, Princess Di," he said gruffly. "Am I disturbing you?"

Only her pulse rate, she thought. Oh, that voice, that magnificent voice. "No, of course not."

"Is the cat feeling better?"

"Feeling better?" she repeated.

"Well, I figure that any cat who sneezed like that one had to have a nasty cold."

"Oh. Well, the cat is fine. Just dandy. It was nice of you to inquire, though." She couldn't handle this! They had to get off the subject of the cat.

"Well, you're . . . fond of that cat, aren't you?" Spence asked. Cat, hell, he fumed. The Sneezer was a man.

Spence wasn't talking about a mangy cat, Tricia thought, pressing her hand to her forehead. Oh, mercy, what should she say? "Fond? No, I don't know him, the cat, well enough to be what you would call fond of him. We're not that closely acquainted." How's that? she asked herself. Terrific? Lousy? She had absolutely no idea.

"I see," Spence said.

He did? Well, she was glad someone was following this screwy conversation.

"I've got to go, Tricia," he said. "I should be at your place by, say, seven tomorrow night. Okay?"

"Yes, more than okay. I'm looking forward to it."

"Good night."

" 'Night, Spence," she said softly. *I love you, Spence*, she whispered in her mind, and her heart echoed the message.

The next morning Tricia went to Shawna's office before going to her own.

"Hi," Shawna said. "Did you come to borrow back your sugar?"

"No. Is your boss in?"

"Nope. What's up? You don't look too thrilled with life. Or is that exhaustion I see after a passionate weekend with your hunk of stuff Spence?"

"Spence is in Colorado Springs," Tricia said, sinking onto a chair.

"Oh, and you're pining away." Shawna covered her heart with her hand, "That is just so romantic, Tricia. Spence is absolutely gorgeous. I'm going to turn green and die."

"Shawna, you're so dramatic it's ridiculous." Tricia laughed, then frowned. "Have you ever been in love?"

"Once. It was eight years ago. I was twenty years old and dumb as a post about men. Oh, how I loved that idiot. I would have followed him to the end of the earth."

"What happened?"

"He failed to mention the trivial detail called a wife. What a bum. Are you asking because you're in love with Spence?"

"Yes," Tricia said, sighing, "I am. He cares for me, I know he does, but he isn't ready to settle down, to make a commitment."

"Oh, one of those," Shawna said knowingly. "There's a bucketful of that type out there. They're dandy for affairs, Tricia, but you're not supposed to fall in love with them."

"Too late," she said miserably.

"Not good. But you never know. Spence may change his mind, decide he can't live without you. Of course, it wouldn't hurt to nudge him in that direction. Use every ounce of femme fatale you have. Oh, and feel free to cheat. Pull out all the stops."

"Well," Tricia said, shifting in her chair, "I am cheating, sort of forcing a showdown. Spence thinks I'm seeing another man while he's in Colorado Springs. We're playing dumb word games on the phone about the cat sneezing when both of us know it was a man, not a cat. Well, a boy. Freddy, actually, but Spence doesn't know that. So I'm letting him think I'm seeing another man, but I'm not very good at this type of thing, and I'm a nervous wreck. I've practically OD'd on butterscotch balls. Shawna, why is your mouth open?"

Shawn snapped her mouth closed, then shook her head as if to clear it. "Well," she said, "that was quite a dissertation, the gist of which, I think, is that you're trying to make Spence jealous. Right?"

"Oh, Shawna," Tricia said, throwing up her hands, "I don't know what to do. If things go on as they are, Spence will leave me when his internal alarm clock goes off. At least this way I feel as though I'm fighting for him."

"Good for you," Shawna said. "Give him hell. Good luck, Tricia. From where I'm sitting, Spence Walker is a great catch. Besides, if you fell in love with him, he has to be special."

"Thanks, Shawna," Tricia said, getting to her feet. "I'll talk to you later."

"I'll want a daily report," Shawna called after her as Tricia left the office.

At five-thirty that evening Spence slipped behind a parked truck and watched as Tricia came out of her office building and crossed the parking lot. As she drove away, he quickly got into his own car, and a minute later was following her through the rush hour traffic. His little voice was telling him that he was a liar and a louse, and he thoroughly agreed.

But, he rationalized, he was also a desperate man. He was trying frantically to come to grips with the complexities of being in love, to override his own fears and find some peace within himself. He loved Tricia, but he couldn't tell her that, ask her to marry him, until he knew if he was capable of coping with the tempestuous emotion.

And in the meantime? He could very well lose her to another man! The Sneezer was real. He'd been in Tricia's cottage. But Spence knew, he just knew, The Sneezer hadn't been in Tricia's bed. Why he was so sure of that didn't make sense, but there was no doubt in his mind. Tricia had not gone to bed with The Sneezer.

Spence sent mental messages to Tricia to go straight home, then felt the knot in his gut twist painfully when she made a turn in the wrong direction.

"No blinkers," he muttered. "She still hasn't gotten them fixed. I ought to write her up a ticket."

When she pulled into the parking lot of a movie theater, he drove to the next entrance and around to the back. He got out of his car and sneaked along behind her as she walked across the lot.

She was so lovely, he thought. And, oh, Lord, how he loved her. But why was she going to the movies now? He'd told her he'd be at the cottage by seven.

The Sneezer! She had to be meeting The Sneezer. Dammit, he couldn't handle this!

He stiffened, every muscle in his body tensing as she rapped three times on a door at the side of the building. As she waited his fury reached the boiling point, and he curled his hands into tight fists.

The door opened and a man wearing a uniform stepped out.

Tricia smiled at him and Spence's teeth began to ache from the pressure of his clenched jaw.

"Hi, Freddy," she said. "Oh, you look super in your uniform, but you really should stand up straighter to show it off better."

Freddy sighed and straightened his shoulders.

Spence's mouth dropped open.

"Now then," Tricia went on, pulling a large envelope from her bag, "I went over to the chef school on my lunch hour and got this for you. It's an application to take the scholarship exam. Fill it out and mail it right back in so your place will be reserved."

"Okay. Thanks for getting it for me."

"No problem. Do you have any shoe polish? You really should spruce up those shoes to go with the spiffy uniform."

"You're absolutely right," Freddy said wearily. "Whatever you say, Tricia. You name it, I'll do it."

"Is something wrong?" she asked in concern.

"No. No," he said, waving a hand breezily in the air. "You've blown every fuse in my brain, but other than that I'm perfectly fine."

"You're so cute," she said, laughing. "Talk to you soon."

"I'm sure you will," he said, leaning against the building and closing his eyes. He didn't move as Tricia drove out of the parking lot.

Spence's mind was racing so fast he was having difficulty keeping up with his own thoughts. Freddy? Freddy Jackson was the one who wanted to be a chef? Sleazeball Freddy? Spence had hardly recognized him with his hair cut and wearing the theater uniform, but it was the junior hood, all right. What in hell was going on? What was Tricia doing mixed up with Freddy? And Freddy wanted to be a chef? It was time for some answers.

He strode toward Freddy, who was still leaning against the building. Stopping directly in front of the boy, Spence cleared his throat. Freddy's eyes popped open.

"Hello, Freddy," Spence said.

Freddy lunged forward, grabbing Spence's jacket. "Oh, Walker, thank God you're back. You've got to save me from her. I can't take any more of this. She's nice, great, wonderful, but she's driving me crazy! You've got to help me, man. I'll be a perfect citizen. I won't even jaywalk. But, Walker, please call her off. Do something. I'm reformed, I swear it. I'll stand up straight, I'll polish my shoes, I'll do anything. Just get Tricia Todd off my case!"

"One question," Spence said, narrowing his eyes. "Were you at Tricia's the other night when I called? Did you sneeze?"

"Yeah. Yeah, we were studying. I'm going to take an exam to try to get a scholarship to be a chef. I was messing around with her plant and I sneezed. She was ready to murder me. Then she told you the cat had sneezed. Jeez, how stupid does she think you are?"

That did it. Spence laughed. He put his head back and roared. Freddy inched away from him, eyeing him warily as Spence laughed until he was gasping for breath.

"Good Lord," he said finally, grinning and shaking his head. "I don't believe this. I really thought . . . So, Tricia decided to reform you, huh?"

"Yeah. She showed up at Juvenile the day of my hearing."

"Wait a minute. Was she wearing a huge trench coat and a floppy hat?"

"Yeah. She looked like a bag lady."

"I love it," Spence said, chuckling. "She's really something."

"No joke. Look, Walker. Up front, okay? I went along with Tricia's do-gooder number at first because I knew you'd hate it. I was trying to get back at you through her. But then it all changed. Tricia cares, she really cares about me, about you. I've never met anyone like her before."

"I haven't either, Freddy," Spence said quietly.

"I'm grateful to her, I really am. But, oh, man, I'm at the end of the line. I swear, I worry about where my elbows are when I'm sleeping!"

"She's tough, huh?"

"I'm dying! I don't want to hurt her feelings, though. She's been so damn good to me. She told me that wherever I went when I became a chef she'd never forget me. She said I'd be . . . I'd be one of her memories to keep. Can you believe that? It blew my mind."

"I believe it," Spence said, smiling. "She's quite a lady. My lady. Look, I'll handle this, but you'll have to be patient while I figure out the best way to do it. Just go along with Tricia until I get back to you. Don't let on that anything has changed."

"I can't take much more. I'm near the edge now."

"Hang in there," Spence said, clapping him on the shoulder.

"Yeah," Freddy said, sighing. "Right."

Spence walked away, then he stopped. "Freddy," he said, grinning at him over his shoulder.

"Yeah?"

"Stand up straight."

Freddy moaned and buried his face in his hands.

Eight

As Spence turned onto Tricia's street, he thought the summer sky looked as if it had been decorated with fluffy mounds of tinted whipped cream. He remembered that other sunset he had watched with Tricia. There had been a tranquility, a peace within him that night as they'd sat together on her front step.

He loved her so much. And now he knew there was no other man. Tricia was his, his alone.

The smile that had been on his lips all the way from the theater faded slowly, and his grip tightened on the steering wheel. Now, he realized, there was nothing standing between him and Tricia, no reason for him not to declare his love, ask her to marry him, make a lifelong commitment to her.

No reason except his own fear, his chilling fear of love.

Damn, he thought, pounding his fist on the steering wheel. What in hell was wrong with him?

He was a grown man, a realist who knew life at its worst. He should be rejoicing that he was being given the chance to embrace it at its best.

But still he hated that he was defenseless against the pain and heartbreak of love gone wrong. He was placing himself, heart, mind, and soul, in Tricia's hands. Where was his protection? What did a man hold back as a shield against being at the mercy of another?

Granted, as a cop there was no guarantee he'd be alive one day to the next. But he had a fighting chance! He had training that gave him an upper hand.

But love was larger than life, more powerful than anything he had ever known, and, dammit, it was scary as hell.

He pulled in behind Tricia's car in her driveway and turned off the ignition. Folding his arms over the top of the steering wheel, he gazed up at the vibrant sky. Suddenly, her front door opened and Tricia stepped out onto the porch. In the next instant Spence was out of his car and moving toward her, his long legs not covering the ground fast enough to bring her into his arms.

She ran toward him, a bright smile on her face, and he opened his arms to welcome her.

"Spence," she said, and literally flung herself against him.

He caught her high on his chest, crushing her to him as her feet dangled above the ground.

"Oh, Spence."

Their lips met. The heat from their bodies wove together, igniting their passion. He slowly slid her down his body until her feet touched the ground, his mouth never leaving hers. She leaned against him, feeling his arousal and trembling with her own.

With a throaty groan he tore his mouth from hers. He lifted her into his arms and carried her into the house, into the bedroom. . . . He set her on her feet, then shook his head as if coming out of a trance.

After their frenzied lovemaking they lay exhausted on the bed, tucked close together. Spence's throat felt strangely tight as Tricia smiled at him warmly. Her cheeks were rosy with the aftermath of passion.

"Hello," she whispered.

He chuckled. "Hello. I think we forgot to say that."

"It didn't seem important at the time."

"Did I hurt you, Tricia? I was . . . a little impatient."

"No. Did I hurt you?"

He smiled. "No."

"I missed you, Spence," she said, trailing her fingertips through the curly hair on his chest.

"I missed you too."

"Did the trial go the way you hoped?"

"Yep. We nailed him."

She looked directly into his blue eyes. "I love you, Spence. I just need to say it sometimes. I love *only* you. Do you believe that?"

She was asking him to forget about The Sneezer, he realized. He had wondered how she was going to handle that. Should he tell her he knew about Freddy? And admit he'd followed her like a jealous fool? No thanks, he'd pass. She'd confess about

Freddy when she was ready. Jackson would just have to grin and bear it for a while. It would do him a world of good.

"Spence?"

"Yes, I believe that you love me, and that I'm the only man in your life."

"Thank you." Oh, glory be, she thought, cancel World War III. Spence wasn't going to pursue the issue of who the man was who had sneezed. Why he was dropping it she didn't know, but she was definitely counting her blessings. "I love you so much."

Tell her, Spence's little voice whispered. Tell her you love her too.

No! he answered himself back. Not yet. He wasn't ready yet. He couldn't just hand her his soul on a silver platter to do with as she fancied. Yes, she loved him but . . . Damn, it was all so confusing. And so frightening.

"Spence, you're crushing me," she said, wiggling in his tightened embrace.

"What? Oh, I'm sorry."

"Is something wrong?"

"No. No, everything is fine. Let's shower, then go get something to eat. We'll take your car."

"My car? Why?"

"Because I know a cop who's going to write you up a ticket if you don't get your blinker lights fixed."

"Oh. Say, Lieutenant, how about going out to dinner after we take a shower? We'll take my car, and get my blinker lights fixed on the way."

"Good idea," he said, chuckling. "I'm glad you thought of it."

Darkness had settled over the city by the time Tricia and Spence had tended to the blinker lights and driven to a rustic restaurant that specialized in fish. With the night had come a cloud cover that hid the stars and moon. As Spence pulled open the door to the restaurant, he glanced at the sky and realized his mood now matched that dark, unyielding expanse.

While they ate, Spence listened as Tricia chatted on about her new plants, her mother's latest outrageous names for Kathy's baby, and the fact that she was so glad he was back from Colorado Springs.

Had he done that? he wondered incredulously. Had he brought that smile to her lips, such happiness to her beautiful dark eyes? Because she loved him, he had the ability to make Tricia smile. But the flip side of the coin was that it meant he could make her cry.

The power she held over him, he now realized, he also held over her. She gave him her heart and soul, and he gave her his. Lord, it was insane! What seven kinds of fools set themselves up to be blown away like this by love? He couldn't do this. No way.

"Spence, what's wrong?" Tricia asked quietly. "Your teeth are going to crumble if you clench your jaw any tighter. This isn't going to work, is it?"

"What do you mean?" he asked.

"Our pretending you didn't hear that man sneeze when you phoned me."

"Oh, that," he said carelessly. He had feared for a moment that she'd read his mind.

"Yes, that." She took a deep breath. "Okay, here I go. Spence, that was Freddy Jackson you heard sneeze. He was there because I'm reforming him, helping him get back on track. And helping him go after his dream. He wants to be a chef, Spence. Oh, he's a wonderful cook, and he's smart. He's learning so quickly, and I just know he has a chance at the scholarship to the chef school. He's a bit poky about remembering to stand up straight but—"

"Tricia."

"Please don't be angry, Spence. Freddy is a fine, decent young man. I know I was sneaky about this, but I wanted so much to help him. He got a haircut and job, and he hasn't been near the street gang. If you would just talk to him, you'd see that he's not a scum like you thought."

"Okay."

"Pardon me?"

"Okay, I'll talk to him and find out what wonder cure you worked on him."

"You're not going to pitch a fit because I was sneaking around behind your back to help him?"

"No."

"Why not?" she asked, squinting at him.

"You've pointed out to me on more than one occasion that you have the right to make your own choices. Freddy is obviously important to you and I have to respect your decision to try to help him. I'll talk to him. But, Tricia? There are decisions that *I* have the right to make too."

He was no longer talking about Freddy, she thought worriedly. He'd shifted the subject to them. Oh, dear heaven, what was he trying to say, trying to prepare her for? Was this it? The end, the good-bye? No, oh, please no. Oh, Spence.

"I think I'd better take you home," he said. His voice flat.

"You haven't finished your dinner."

"I'm not very hungry."

She searched his face for a clue to what was wrong, but his expression was blank. They didn't speak as they left the restaurant, and she could feel the tension emanating from him.

"I'll just pick up my car when we get to your place," he said finally.

"You're not staying?"

"I wouldn't be very good company tonight, Tricia. I'm tired. No, that's not true, I'm not tired. I just need some time alone to think things through."

"Things? What things? Why can't we talk about what's troubling you, sort it through together?"

"Don't do your 'why' number now," he said gruffly. "I need to be alone, that's all."

It was falling apart, she thought, feeling the ache of tears in her throat. She was losing him. Just hours before they had been making love, such beautiful love together, and now he was a breath away from walking out of her life. Why? She didn't understand. She'd told him the truth about Freddy and he hadn't been angry. Dammit, why was he doing this? Had his internal alarm clock gone off? Why didn't he say something? Didn't he know how much his silence hurt?

Spence's head was pounding with a steadily increasing pain. He felt strangely disoriented, and his thoughts were jumbled. He glanced at Tricia and felt as though a knife were twisting inside him. He knew he was hurting her, and was filled with self-loathing. But he couldn't explain to her something that he didn't understand himself. Nothing was clear to him except the driving need to flee, to be alone.

"I'll see you in," he said when she had parked in her driveway.

Just like a date, she thought almost hysterically. Thank you for a lovely time and I'll call you. This wasn't happening. She was having a nightmare, and would open her eyes and find Spence sleeping peacefully beside her. No, it was real.

Spence didn't speak or touch her as they walked to her front door, and she felt cold, so cold she might never again be warm.

In the living room she turned to face him. She wouldn't cry, she thought. She'd never speak to herself again if she cried. Her world was crumbling into a million pieces, but she wasn't going to cry in front of Spence.

"Tricia—" he started, then stopped to take a deep breath. "Tricia, I know I owe you an explanation for my behavior, but I can't give you one right now. Maybe I'll never . . . be able to explain. I don't know."

"No," she said. She lifted her chin and prayed her voice remained steady. "You don't owe me anything, Spence. We made no commitments to each other. You never even—even said you loved me to give me false hopes that we might have a future together. You're free to leave whenever you choose. You've apparently picked this moment to do that."

"It's not like that," he said, an almost frantic edge to his voice. "I need to think. I need . . . Hell,

I don't know what I need. If I could explain it to you, I would, but I don't understand it myself. It's the fear. The fear of . . ." He raked a hand through his hair. "It's all a jumbled mess in my mind, Tricia. I've got to go, don't you see?"

"Then go," she whispered, fighting against her tears. "With my love, Spence, go."

A haunting pain settled in his blue eyes. He took one step toward her, lifting his hand as if to touch her. Then he spun around and left, closing the door hard behind him.

Tricia stared at the door, listening to the screech of tires as Spence drove away. When she could no longer hear his car, she walked as if in a trance into the kitchen. She got a butterscotch ball from the cupboard and looked at the cellophane-wrapped candy as it lay in her palm. Then she curled her fingers tightly around it. The sharp pain of her nails digging into her skin shocked her back into reality.

"Oh, Spence," she said, nearly choking on a sob. "I've lost you. I've lost you to something I don't even understand."

She gave way to her tears. She cried loud and long. She got a roaring headache, a red nose, puffy eyes, but she didn't care. She cried because she was incredibly sad, because she was lonely, frustrated, angry, and confused. She cried because Spence was gone and she didn't know why. She cried until she was drained of energy, and had a terrible case of the hiccups.

And then, for lack of anything better to do, she ate the butterscotch ball.

• • •

It came as no surprise to Tricia that she had difficulty sleeping that night, nor was she particularly upset when she glanced at her reflection in the mirror the next morning and saw the shadows beneath her eyes.

As she drank her coffee she told the creeping Charlie that Spence Walker was a rotten bum for having left her without telling her why. He was a colossal rat, she informed the Boston fern, and deserved to be shot in the dingle-dangle. He was a cad—and she missed him more with every breath she took.

Broken hearts, she decided, as she drove to her office, were not fun.

At noon, after a nonproductive morning that had consisted of a great many sighs, Tricia locked her office and headed for the elevator. She absolutely did *not* want to see Shawna. One sympathetic word, just one, was bound to cause her to burst into fresh tears.

She walked the three blocks to a small park nestled among the tall buildings, where she was to meet Freddy and quiz him further for the exam.

"Hi," he said, getting up from a bench as she approached.

"Hi," she said, managing a weak smile. "I brought us some sandwiches."

They settled onto the bench. Tricia produced the lunch from her tote bag, then opened the book on her lap. "Before we start, Freddy," she said, "I should tell you that I told Spence about what you and I are doing."

"And?"

She shrugged. "And nothing. He didn't even

seem that surprised. And he certainly wasn't angry. He promised me he'd come speak to you, see for himself that you're on the right track. Of course, maybe he won't now that he—" She sniffled. "He . . . um . . ." She looked down at the book. "What's a scallion?"

"A bulbless onion. What's wrong, Tricia? What did Walker do to you?"

"He left me!" she wailed, and burst into tears.

"What in the hell for?" Freddy roared, jumping to his feet.

"I don't know," she said, dabbing at her nose with a tissue. "Sit down. Sit up straight, but sit down."

He plunked himself back onto the bench. "Are you sure that Walker wasn't ticked off at you for helping me?"

"Positive. This has nothing to do with you, Freddy, I swear it. I shouldn't have dumped on you this way, but it just snuck up on me, and I'm so miserable, and I love him so much. I'm sorry. I'm a wreck. Let's just study, okay?"

"No." He took the book from her and snapped it closed. "My mom will help me, and my sisters too. I'll pass that exam with flying colors, you'll see. You don't have to worry about me anymore, Tricia. I'm reformed from head to toe. You just concentrate on yourself now."

"Are you sure?"

"Yeah. I'll polish my shoes, stand straight as a stick, and I'll let you know the minute I get the results of the exam. Okay?"

"Well, I—I guess so, if you're really sure that you're all set."

"No doubt about it, and I owe it all to you. I wish there was some way to repay you for what you've done for me."

"Just get that scholarship," she said, smiling. She stood up. "Good luck, Freddy. I'll have my fingers and toes crossed for you on the day of the exam. Call me the minute you know anything."

"I will."

" 'Bye."

" 'Bye," he called after her as she walked away. "I owe you, Tricia," he added quietly, "and I'm going to pay up."

At eleven o'clock that night Ted Baker slid into a booth in a dimly lit bar and frowned at Spence Walker.

"Don't you have a home to go to?" Spence asked, barely glancing at his friend.

"Don't you?"

"No. I have an apartment. An empty apartment. Big difference between the two, buddy. How'd you know I was here?"

"Rosie called me. She said she'd just served you your fourth double Scotch, and she figured you had troubles. Besides that, she wasn't sure what she was going to do with you when you passed out."

"I'm not drunk."

"But you're close, pal, very close. I've never seen you drink like this, Spence. Where's your gun?"

"Locked in the car."

"In other words, you'd made up your mind to get blitzed when you came in here."

Spence shrugged and took a deep swallow of his drink. Ted leaned back against the leather booth and crossed his arms over his chest. Several minutes ticked by as a twangy love song played on the jukebox and an occasional burst of laughter sounded from somewhere across the room.

"How's Tricia?" Ted finally asked.

Spence opened his mouth, then shut it, shook his head, and drained the glass.

"Well?" Ted said. "How is she? How's Tricia?"

"Buzz off," Spence said, signaling to Rosie for another drink. "Go home to your wife and baby, Ted. That's where you belong."

"And where do you belong? Here? Getting sloshed? Why aren't you with the woman you love?"

"I never said I—"

"Can it!" Ted said. He pounded the table with his fist and Spence blinked in surprise. Rosie approached the table with Spence's drink, but Ted waved her away. "Dammit, Spence, you love Tricia Todd, right?"

Spence slouched back in the booth. "Yeah."

"Does she love you?"

"Yeah."

"Oh, well," Ted said dryly, "that explains your sunshine mood. The woman you love loves you. Rotten situation."

"Sunshine. That's Tricia," Spence said, his words starting to slur. "Sunshine."

"Come on, Spence. What gives?"

"I left her, walked out, never told her I loved her. I bet she cried. Damn, I bet she did. Oh, Lord, my head hurts."

"Why?"

"Because I'm drunk."

"No, not why does your head hurt. Why did you leave her? Why didn't you tell her that you love her?"

"Why? That's Tricia's favorite question. She always asks why. It's so cute how she does that. Why, Spence, she'd say and—"

"Dammit, Walker, talk to me. Why did you leave her?"

"Because—because I'm scared to death, Teddy."

"You? Of what?"

"Of . . . love. Of being in love, of laying it all on the line. Hell, there's no defense against the pain if it goes bad, don't you see? Tricia has the power to blow me away. What do I say? Here's my soul, lady. Here's my heart. Try not to smash them to smithereens, okay?"

"It's not like that, Spence."

"Isn't it? I say it is."

"You get as much as you give. Love is sharing. You have the power to hurt her, too, you know, but people in love don't set out to do that. You said Tricia was sunshine, and that's right on the mark. We need them, Spence, these women who love us, because we work in a stinking, dark world. My wife is my life. There's nothing to fear or lose by loving, Spence. Which would you rather be? In love or in lonely for the rest of your life?"

"In love," Spence repeated slowly. "Or . . . in . . . lonely."

Ted watched in fascination as Spence passed out cold, slid off the booth, and disappeared under the table.

•   •   •

Tricia's gloomy mood hadn't improved by Wednesday. Shawna cornered her in the hall for an update on Spence and Tricia burst into tears. Shawna declared the hunk of stuff was a complete dolt, a space case wasted on a magnificent body.

"Maybe it would have helped if his name were Ernest," Tricia said, sniffling. "That means 'he who is of sincere intent.' Oh, I can't stand this. I've never been so miserable in my entire life. Butterscotch balls don't even calm me down. I'm going to report Spence Walker to his general, or colonel, or whatever it is they have. That man stole my heart and I want it back! And that, Shawna, is the dumbest thing I've ever said."

Shawna couldn't help laughing, but then she gave Tricia a hug.

"Hush, hush," she said. "That's enough tears for the creep. Why don't we go away for the weekend? We'll pamper ourselves, have room service, the whole bit. We'll also flirt with everything in pants."

"I don't think so," Tricia said, brushing the tears from her cheeks. "I'll just stay home and brood. I'm getting very proficient at it."

"Shame on you," Shawna said, clicking her tongue. "No man is worth this much heartache."

"Spence Walker is!" Tricia wailed. And the tears started once again.

Near midnight on Thursday, Spence walked slowly across the parking lot of the police station toward his car. He had no desire to go home, but he sure as hell wasn't going to a bar. He was never, ever drinking again.

Suddenly the hairs on the back of his neck prickled and his little voice whispered that he should be paying attention to what was happening around him.

He quickly looked around and saw a shadowy figure moving among the trees lining the edge of the parking lot. In the next instant Spence's gun was in his hand.

"Show yourself," he said loudly. "Move into the light. Now!"

Hands shot up straight into the air as the figure hurried into a bright circle of light in the parking lot.

"Freddy!" Spence said. He tucked his gun back into his belt and walked over to the boy. "What the hell are you doing here?"

"I've been waiting for you. I need to talk to you."

"So talk. I'm listening."

"It's none of my business, but it's sorta my business because I care about her and—oh, dammit, Walker, why did you have to go and make Tricia so sad? You gotta do something, man. I can't stand to see her ripped up like this. Why did you leave her, Walker? Why?"

Nine

Why?

That insidious word had been beating against Spence's brain relentlessly. Ted had asked him why while Spence had been in his drunken stupor, and now Freddy was demanding an answer to that question. Spence had no choice but to face once again his inner turmoil, to admit to himself the weakness that was keeping him from Tricia.

He was filled with a sudden fury, a driving need to grab Freddy by the shirt and slam him against the car. He wanted to rage in anger at the boy, tell him to back off, leave him alone. Freddy was a scum, and he was stepping over the wrong line. How dare the punk intrude in his life and—

"Go ahead," Freddy said quietly.

"What?" Spence asked.

"You want to deck me. I can tell. Go ahead,

Walker, lay me out, but it won't change anything. Tricia will still be sad, she'll still be crying."

"Crying?" The word seemed to stick in his throat.

"Yeah. Crying. What's really ripping her up is that she doesn't know why you walked out on her. I thought you might be ticked because she was helping me get it together, but she said you weren't. I'd already seen you at the theater and you didn't seem uptight about it. I guess the bottom line must be that you just don't love her like she loves you. How you couldn't love her, I sure as hell don't know, but you owe her an answer, a reason for leaving. You really do."

As he listened to Freddy's softly spoken words, Spence watched the emotions play across the boy's face. Gone was the belligerent, cocky kid with the mile-high chip on his shoulder. Freddy was speaking from his heart as a man. Speaking from a heart that had been touched by Tricia Todd.

"You've really changed, Freddy," Spence said.

"I'm reformed," he said, smiling slightly. "All my life I've been trying to be so much to so many people. My mom, my sisters. I always fell short because I couldn't earn enough money to really help, I wasn't old enough to make a difference. They all looked to me to make things better, but I couldn't do it."

"That wasn't your fault."

"No, but I felt lousy all the time. They didn't mean to put that kind of pressure on me, but it was there, eating at me. Then Tricia came along. I've never known anyone like her. She gives and gives, and you know what she asks for in return? Nothing. She really wants me to get the scholarship to chef school. For me, Walker. Just for me. There's nothing in it for her. Not a damn thing."

Spence nodded and shoved his hands into his jacket pockets, his gaze riveted on Freddy's face.

"Tricia deserves the best life has," Freddy went on. "I didn't think she had such terrific taste in men when I found out how much she loved you. Jeez, a cop. And you're a mean, tough cop to boot. But when I saw her face light up when you called her, or when she talked about you, I figured there must be more to you than I thought. Obviously, there isn't."

Spence stiffened and narrowed his eyes. "Now, look—"

"No, you look," Freddy said, his voice rising. "What are you made of, Walker? Stone? Do you know what Tricia gave me? Myself. My self-esteem, a belief in me. That's a gift from her, a kind of love I can never repay. For you? Man, for you she's got it all. The big-time stuff, the forever stuff. And you're throwing it down the drain! Know what she'd ask from you in return? Nothing. All you'd have to do is be there, and love her."

"Freddy . . ."

"Dammit, you're sick," Freddy said, backing up as his eyes filled with tears. "You don't deserve Tricia's love. You wouldn't know heaven if you tripped over it. Okay, fine, throw her away, turn your back on her, have a wonderful time playing the big cop all alone. But, damn you, give her a reason, tell her why. Don't let her go on crying, Walker!"

"I—"

"Go to hell," Freddy said, then turned and ran, disappearing into the darkness of the trees.

"I'm already there, Freddy," Spence said quietly, and with weary steps, feeling as though the last ounce of energy had drained from his body, he walked to his car.

Late Friday afternoon, as she washed out the coffeepot at her office, Tricia wondered if she should have taken Shawna up on the offer of going away for the weekend. In the next instant she dismissed the thought, deciding it would have been masochistic to plunk herself in the middle of a couples-oriented society. She'd just stay home, talk to her plants, and say hello to Cat if he dropped by for dinner.

"How thrilling," she muttered. "I don't know if I can take all that excitement."

With a sigh she hoisted her tote bag onto her shoulder. She turned out the lights and opened the door, then stopped and stared down at the floor with wide eyes.

Placed inches apart in a neat line was a seemingly endless row of butterscotch balls.

"I can't afford a psychiatrist," she muttered. "It's really not in my budget." She stepped carefully over the candy, pulled her door closed, and locked it. Glancing around to make sure no one was watching, she started down the hall, walking next to the trail of cellophane-wrapped treats. "I'm definitely out of my mind."

As she approached the elevator, she groaned as she saw a group of people staring at the candy.

They were talking among themselves, several shrugging and shaking their heads.

"Coming through," she called out. "Step aside, please. There's an official research project being conducted here. Step aside."

"What kind of research project?" a man asked.

"Really, sir," Tricia said, "I'm not at liberty to say. It's classified top secret."

"By the feds? This is the way they're spending my taxes? I'll sue."

"Step aside. Step aside," she said, waving her hands in the air.

Much to her amazement, the group moved quickly back, making her feel like Moses after parting the Red Sea. She ignored the man who declared three more times that he was going to sue for misuse of his taxes and went blissfully on her way, pursuing the trail of butterscotch balls.

It took her to the door leading to the stairs.

She pulled the door open with the intention of peering cautiously around it before proceeding, but a quick glance back toward the elevator told her that the group was watching every move she made. With a tingle of excitement and a determined lift of her chin she swooped inside the stairwell, making what she decided had been an extremely classy and dramatic exit from the hallway.

The butterscotch balls marched precisely across the landing to the stairs leading down to the third floor. She walked to the top of the stairs and stared in amazement. There they were, three candies to each step, beckoning onward.

A bubble of laughter escaped from her as she

started down the stairs. Who in the world had gone to so much trouble to create this strange treasure hunt? she wondered. Everyone she knew teased her about her weakness for butterscotch balls, and she could think of several friends who were wacky enough to invent the game, Shawna included.

She scampered down the stairs feeling more lighthearted than she had in days. Than she had since Spence had left her.

The candy continued across the third floor landing and down the stairs. She shrugged and started off again, then stopped.

The butterscotch-ball trail ended on the second step down, right in front of Spence Walker.

"Hello, Tricia," he said.

"Spence," she gasped. "What . . . why . . ."

"Why?" He smiled slightly. "That familiar word. Because I was afraid if I came to your office or your house you'd refuse to see me. I was hoping you couldn't resist the lure of butterscotch balls."

"But . . ."

He came up to the landing and shoved his hands into his back pockets.

"This is where I first saw you," he said. "There you were, pointing your squirt gun at Freddy." He paused. "A lot has happened since that day."

"Yes. Yes, it has," she said, unable to tear her gaze from his face. He looked tired, she thought. Why was he here? What did he want? Oh, he was so beautiful, and she loved him so much. He couldn't hear how wildly her heart was beating, could he? Maybe she'd better scoop up a handful of those butterscotch balls and stuff them into her mouth.

"I'd like to talk to you, Tricia. I know I don't have the right to ask any favors after the way I walked out on you, but I *am* asking. May I follow you home? Please?"

Certainly not, she thought indignantly. Did he assume she had a revolving door on her house and her heart? The nerve of the man to just waltz back into her life. She had no intention of sitting down for a cozy chat with Lieutenant Spencer Walker.

"Tricia?"

"Yes, of course," she said. "Follow me home."

"Thank you."

"I'm taking the elevator." She pulled open the door to the hall. "I'll see you there. 'Bye."

"I'll be right behind you, sunshine," he said.

As she drove home, Tricia's hands were trembling so badly she gripped the steering wheel until her fingers ached. Her mind was whirling with unanswered questions.

Why? she kept asking herself. Why had Spence suddenly reappeared? Why . . . No, she wouldn't think or she'd have a nervous breakdown before she had a chance to hear what he had to say.

He was waiting on the porch when she arrived and she willed her rubbery legs to carry her from the car to the house. He stepped back but didn't speak as she unlocked the door. Inside, he wandered around the room, stopping to trail his finger along a shiny leaf of the creeping Charlie. He shoved his hands into the back pockets of his jeans, pulled them out again, then stared at the Boston fern.

He was nervous, Tricia thought incredulously. Mean, lean, tough Spence Walker was nervous. Not that she was in terrific shape herself, but it was amazing that Spence was nervous.

She sank onto the sofa and watched him walk slowly toward her. He stopped about three feet away and looked down at her, a deep frown on his face.

"I like that dress," he said. Great opening, Walker, he thought.

"Thank you," she said. Why was he talking about her dress?

"Tricia," he said, raking a hand through his hair, "I'm so sorry for the way I just disappeared. It was a lousy thing to do."

"Yes, it was."

He appeared startled for a moment. "Oh . . . right. But, Tricia, that night, the night I left you, everything was all jumbled together in my mind and I couldn't sort it out. I felt as if I couldn't breathe, as if I were shoved up against a wall and it was all closing in on me."

"What was closing in on you, Spence?" she asked, her voice shaky.

He took a deep breath and stared at the ceiling for a long moment. Her heart battered wildly against her ribs.

"Love," he finally said, looking back at her. "Your love for me . . ."

"Oh, Spence," she said, then gave up trying to speak as a sob caught in her throat.

"And," he went on, "my—my love for you."

The air seemed to swish from Tricia's lungs and a roaring noise filled her ears.

"Your love for—" she began hesitantly.

Spence shoved his hands into his back pockets again. "Tricia, I love you," he said, his voice breaking. "But . . ."

Tears misted her eyes. But what? she wondered. Oh, dear God, what? He loved her! Spence loved her, but what?

"Tricia, I've lived with fear all of my adult life. It's part of being a cop. My father taught me that that fear was healthy, had kept him alive while he wore the uniform, and would keep me sharp, alert. That kind of fear was my companion, was even sometimes a little warning voice inside me. I welcomed that fear."

"Yes," she said, nodding, "I understand."

"I told myself that I would marry someday, when I was ready and the time was right. No problem, I said, it's just a matter of reaching the point where I was prepared to settle down. I was playing mind games with myself, and I didn't even know it. And then, there you were, turning my life upside down. My world changed from the moment I saw you pointing that squirt gun at Freddy and threatening to shoot him in the dingle-dangle."

"I still can't believe I actually said that," she muttered. "Go on, Spence. I'm listening to every word."

"I told myself to stay away from you," he continued, beginning to pace the floor, "but I couldn't do it. I felt protective, even possessive toward you right from the start."

"How sweet," she said, smiling. He glared at her. "Sorry," she said. "Carry on."

"I also told myself that I was not, *absolutely was not*, going to make love to you." He threw his hands up. "But I did."

"You certainly did," she said, and sighed. "Mercy."

"Dammit, Tricia, pay attention!"

"I am!"

"Good. Then then I fell in love with you. But . . ."

"But?"

He stopped his pacing to stand in front of her again. His voice was quiet when he spoke.

"With that love came a fear like nothing I had ever experienced before. I saw myself robbed of my strength, my ability to defend myself against potential heartache. Love was an equalizer, leaving me vulnerable, stripped of all I had to protect myself. I envisioned that I was giving you my heart and soul to do with as you would. And into *my* hands came *your* heart and soul, and I didn't know what to do with them! I didn't want to be in love, Tricia. It scared the hell out of me, and I couldn't handle it."

"So you left me," she whispered. "Oh, Spence, why didn't you explain, tell me what you were feeling, what you were going through?"

"I couldn't! It all jammed together in my mind, driving me crazy. My pride got in the way too. I realize that now. Tough-cop Walker, scared out of his shorts. How in hell was I supposed to open my mouth and say *that*? I was so damned confused, so I ran. I just turned tail and ran. And, God, how I missed you."

"Oh, Spence," she said, brushing a tear from her cheek.

He resumed his pacing. "Ted talked to me. I was drunk as a skunk at the time, but some of what he said got through. He asked me if I wanted to be in love or in lonely for the rest of my life. I kept thinking and thinking, trying to sort it out. I couldn't do it, Tricia. And then—"

She sat up straighter, her gaze never leaving his face as he trekked back and forth.

"Then Freddy."

"Freddy?" she repeated. "What does Freddy have to do with any of this?"

"I tell you, Tricia, when you reform someone, you don't mess around. That kid is something. He's a man now, with a purpose, a goal. He told me where to put myself for the way I treated you."

"Oh, dear."

"And he was right. But he said more. He talked about you, about how you give so much without asking for anything in return. Love flows from you, just like sunshine, with no strings attached. You loved me, Tricia, and you made no demands. You didn't stand there waiting to collect my heart and soul, the very essence of who I am. You just gave."

"Because I love you," she said softly.

"Freddy, former sleazeball Freddy understands your kind of love. It took a tweaky kid to explain it to hot-dog me. Just be there, he said. Just love Tricia and be there with her. I thought about what he'd said. I went over and over it. I relived every moment I'd been with you since I saw you on those stairs. I'd fallen in love with you and I didn't lose myself. I gained your love. What had been empty within me, you filled. Whatever I gave to you, you returned tenfold. Our loving each other didn't rob me of any part of who I am. It made me complete for the first time in my life. That's how love works, right? A person keeps his own identity, his inner being, and the love is extra, like a precious gift. That's it, isn't it? I've got it figured out now, don't I?"

"Yes!" she said, pushing herself up off the sofa. "Oh, yes, Spence, you do."

"Tricia, I love you," he said, his voice choked with emotion. "I do love you, and I'm so sorry, and I'm begging you to forgive me for hurting you. Share your sunshine with me, share your love. Oh, Tricia, please!"

She flung herself into his arms, wrapping her own arms around his neck and burying her face in his shirt. He held her tightly, nestling his face in her fragrant curls.

"Tricia?"

"Oh, yes, Spence." She tilted her head back to look up at him. "I'll share my love, my life with you. I love you, Spence Walker. I will always love you."

"Will you marry me? Will you be my wife for better, for worse? In good times and bad? I'll never leave you again, I swear it."

"Yes, Spence. Yes, I'll marry you. All I need is you, your love. Just be with me, Spence. Forever."

"Oh, thank God," he said, and kissed her. The kiss was rough at first, an expression of his inner turmoil, his confusion and fear. But then it gentled as the last of the tension ebbed from his body. He drank of Tricia's sweetness, filled his senses with all that she was. Filled his heart and soul with love. "I love you and I want you," he said when he lifted his head.

"And I want you," she said breathlessly. "Welcome home, Spence. Welcome home, my love."

Outside, the last of the sunset melted into darkness, and stars popped out to twinkle a million hellos. The cat meowed at the back door, but when no one answered his summons, he curled up in a ball on the porch, dozing as he waited patiently. Crickets began a serenade to welcome the night. Peace settled over the woods.

Inside the cottage Tricia and Spence became one together, soaring to their private place of ecstasy. They declared their love over and over, making their commitment to a lifetime together.

A lifetime of love and laughter, butterscotch balls and sunshine.

Epilogue

Spence stretched out next to Tricia on the bed where she lay propped against the pillows. He slid his hand to the nape of her neck and brought her lips to his for a long, searing kiss.

"Mercy," she said when he finally released her. "You certainly know how to kiss a person, Spence Walker."

"So do you, Tricia Walker. I do other things rather well too," he added smugly, placing his hand on her protruding stomach.

"Yes, I know," she said, rolling her eyes. "You created that baby all by yourself."

"I'm an amazing man," he said, wiggling his eyebrows. "I have great muscle tone, remember? What did Freddy have to say in his letter?"

"He adores Paris, is learning to speak French so he can dazzle the ladies, and is studying very hard. Oh, Spence, I'm so proud of him. First he won the scholarship to the school here, then six months later they selected him to study on full scholarship in their Paris school. He has a wonderful future ahead of him."

"Thanks to you."

"Oh, no, not me. He's done it all himself." She frowned. "I just hope that he's remembering to stand up straight."

Spence chuckled. "There's the phone," he said, swinging his feet to the floor. "I'll get it."

Tricia reread Freddy's letter, and was smiling when Spence returned to the bedroom and lay down beside her again. "That was your mother on the phone," he said.

"Break it to me gently."

"Well . . ." He trailed his fingers across her stomach. "Today's contribution is as follows. If it's a girl we should name her 'Harriet' which means 'mistress of the home.' "

"Oh, good grief," Tricia said, laughing.

"And if it's a boy he's to be 'Alphonso' for 'prepared for battle' in case he decides to become a cop."

"I think I need a butterscotch ball."

"Nope. You've had your quota. You're addicted to those things."

"No," she said, placing her hand on his cheek, "I'm addicted to you and the happiness you've brought me. I love you so much, Spence."

"And I love you, Tricia. I've decided to keep you."

"Oh, how nice, since I plan to stick around for fifty years or more. While you're keeping me, I wonder if I'll have room in the treasure chest in my heart for all the wonderful memories *I* plan to keep."

"Sure you will. You're very organized."

"Ha. I—oh! Spence?"

"Yeah?"

"I'm about to have a new memory to keep."

"Which is?"

"Of having been pregnant. Harriet-Alphonso is on the way!"

"Oh, good Lord," Spence said, scrambling off the bed. "I need a butterscotch ball!"

THE EDITOR'S CORNER

Seven is supposed to be a lucky number ... so look for luck next month as you plunge into the four delightful LOVESWEPT romances and the second trilogy of the Delaney series. Has the Free Sampler of **THE DELANEYS OF KILLAROO** made you eager to read the full books? (Whenever we do a book sampler I get the most wonderful letters of protest! Many of them very funny.) As you know from the creative promotion we've done with Clairol® to help them launch their new product, PAZAZZ® SHEER COLORWASH will be available next month when the Delaney books, too, are out. Think how much fun it would be to do your own personal make-over in the style of one of the heroines of **THE DELANEYS OF KILLAROO**! *Adelaide, The Enchantress* by Kay Hooper has hair like *Sheer Fire; Matilda, The Adventuress* by Iris Johansen has tresses with the spicy allure of *Sheer Cinnamon; Sydney, The Temptress* by Fayrene Preston has a mystery about her echoed in the depths of her *Sheer Plum* hair color. Enjoy this big three!

And for your four LOVESWEPTS, you start with **A DREAM TO CLING TO**, LOVESWEPT #206. Sally Goldenbaum makes her debut here as a solo author—you'll remember Sally has teamed up in the past with Adrienne Staff—and has created a love story that is filled with tenderness and humor and great passion. Brittany Winters is a generous, spirited woman who believes life should be taken seriously. This belief immediately puts her at odds with the roguishly handsome Sam Lawrence, originator of "Creative Games." Sam is a wanderer, a chaser of dreams ...

(continued)

and a man who is utterly irresistible. (What woman could resist a man who calls her at dawn and tells her to watch the sunrise while he whispers words of love to her?) **A DREAM TO CLING TO** is an enchanting book that we think you will remember for a long time.

PLAYING HARD TO GET, LOVESWEPT #207, is one of Barbara Boswell's most intriguing stories yet. Slade Ramsey is the proverbial nice guy, but, jilted by his fiancee, he got tired of finishing last. Figuring women really did prefer scoundrels, he tried hard to become one. However, he was only playing the part of a charming heartbreaker, and he never got over the love he felt for the first woman he had treated badly— young and innocent Shavonne Brady. When he comes face to face with Shavonne, gazing again into her big brown eyes and seeing the woman she has become, Slade knows he can never leave her again. But how can he convince her that the man she knew a few years ago—the one who had broken her heart—isn't the real Slade? Barbara has written a truly memorable story, and not only will you fall in love with Shavonne and Slade, but all of their brothers and sisters are unforgettable characters as well.

In **KATIE'S HERO** by Kathleen Creighton, LOVE-SWEPT #208, Katherine Taylor Winslow comes face to face with Hollywood's last swashbuckling star, Cole Grayson. Katie is a writer who always falls in love with the heroes of her novels. Now she's doing a biography of Cole . . . and he's the epitome of a hero. How can she fail to fall for him? Katie and her hero are as funny and warmhearted a pair as you're ever likely to find in a romance, and we think you are going to be as amused by Katie as a tenderfoot on Cole's ranch as

(continued)

you are beguiled by the tenderness of a hero who's all man. This book is a real treat!

Only Sara Orwig could turn a shipwreck into a romantic meeting, and she does just that in **VISIONS OF JASMINE,** LOVESWEPT #209. After the ship she and her fellow researchers were on sinks, Jasmine Kirby becomes separated from her friends, alone in her own lifeboat. She is thrilled when she is rescued, but a little dubious about the rescuer—a scruffy sailor with a hunk's body and a glint in his eye that warns her to watch out for her virtue. Matthew Rome is bewitched by Jasmine, and begins to teach her how to kick up her heels and live recklessly. When they meet again in Texas, Jasmine is astounded to discover that the man she'd thought was a charming ne'er do well actually lives a secret and dangerous life.

Four great LOVESWEPTs and three great Delaney Dynasty novels . . . a big Lucky Seven just for you next month.

With every good wish,

Sincerely,

Carolyn Nichols

Carolyn Nichols
  Editor
LOVESWEPT
Bantam Books, Inc.
666 Fifth Avenue
New York, NY 10103

It's a little like being Loveswept

SHEER MADNESS

SHEER COLOR

SHEER PASSION

SHEER EXCITEMENT

SHEER INTRIGUE

SHEER ROMANCE

All it takes is a little imagination and more Pazazz.®

Coming this July from Clairol…Pazazz Sheer Color Wash —8 inspiring sheer washes of color that last up to 4 shampoos.

Look for the Free Loveswept *THE DELANEYS OF KILLAROO* book sampler this July in participating stores carrying Pazazz Sheer Color Wash.

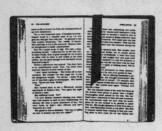